Sgt. Janus

ON THE DARK TRACK

SGT. JANUS ON THE DARK TRACK
©2020 Jim Beard

A Flinch Books Production
Flinch Books and the Flinch Books logo
© Jim Beard and John C. Bruening
www.facebook.com/flinchbooks

Cover illustration and design by Jeffrey Ray Hayes
PlasmaFire Graphics, LLC
www.plasmafiregraphics.com

Interior layout and formatting by Maggie Ryel

ISBN: 978-0-9977903-6-8

*For the Little Woman, whose music haunts
this novel in ways both familiar and unexpected....*
Jim Beard

TABLE OF CONTENTS

Thank you all for being here today. I am glad to see each and every one of you. Though it may not appear so, I've crossed a great distance to be able to address this body this evening. Not figuratively, but literally, and in more ways than one. I also stand before you a changed man, and again, in several ways.

You may have noticed that I've set aside my prepared speech, but I assure you it's only temporarily. Before you become too mystified, or even irritated, I hope to explain myself and return to the planned path.

What has happened is that I've looked out among the faces—your faces—arrayed before me in this grand auditorium, and I am struck by an overwhelming feeling of kinship with each and every one of you, despite our diversity of personality and background. Here is the formidable Miss Van Slyke, Mr. Carnacki, the prince, of course, and our dear friend St. Cyprian—wake up, Charles! There's a good fellow—and so many others whose combined expertise in our chosen profession staggers me. And so, I speak to you now not from notes, but from my heart, my mind, and my experiences on a matter that has in the past year become paramount in my own undertaking of our profession and has informed some of the change of which I have spoken.

To wit: There is much we do not know.

I see you smile and nod your heads—obvious, of course. I understand. But what I mean is that beyond the mysteries we deal with day in and day out lie even deeper questions, questions that make up a larger world, a larger reality that exists even outside of the one we address in our work. And I have seen it.

Some but not all of you may be aware of my nearly year-long absence. Where was I? Where had I gone? Why did I leave and stay away so long? I dearly wish I could answer these questions with exactness, but…I don't know myself. Not completely. But I tell you in all truth and with as much clarity as I can offer that I was elsewhere and—and saw and learned of things that have left me a changed man. Those of you who know me well will hopefully see past the mere words I'm using to realize there is much more I would like to say about my journey if only there was vocabulary to describe it. Maybe someday there will be.

Before I ramble on to the point of inanity, let me leave you with this thought as we work our way through today and tomorrow's programs: Be open to that which you do not already know. Be open to wonder. Be open to larger things. Be open to the idea of humanity as merely the first step upon a grand staircase. Be open to our place in the universe.

And with that, I return to my speech on…

Sgt. Roman Janus
Excerpt from Opening Remarks
One-Hundredth-Twenty-Ninth Conclave of Occupational Occultists

Part One
CHASE

June 9

Dear Diary,

It has been a long time.

Looking back at the last entry I made in you, I see how many years have passed—but since I've found you again and having decided to carry you with me on this trip, waiting for the right time to return to setting down my thoughts, I feel as though that time has arrived. The odd circumstances of the last few hours seem to be noteworthy, and so here I am.

I feel as if I should reintroduce myself. This is Valerie, of course. The last entry I made in you, I see Richard was still alive. He's been gone now for nearly four years and I have accepted that. I was very fond of him, and I think he of me, but we both knew exactly why we were married. After he died and not content to simply be a well-off widow, I threw myself into his business affairs, the restaurant especially, but in the past year I've left it in more capable hands than mine and it seems to be doing well… but, I digress. I should tell you about what has happened today.

Where should I begin? These last few months have been—what have they been? I wish I could say, but suffice to say they have been full; full of life, full of hope, but also full of questions and doubt.

I am with Roman Janus, you see. And as I've said, we are on a trip together.

You remember Roman, don't you? In many ways he's the same man I was once engaged to a lifetime ago, or so it seems. Look back through what I've written to you about him and you'll be reminded of all my hopes and dreams concerning him, which I suppose are childish now. Maybe they were childish then, too. Regardless, we have become reacquainted after all these years and rekindled our…I was about to write "friendship"? Yes, that will do for now. It sounds much better than anything else. We have renewed our friendship and it has meant more to be in the last few months than I ever imagined it could. Roman is an engaging man, as fascinating as ever before and still as handsome, but in that rough way of his and...oh, I should probably get on with it, today's events, or they may drift right out of my brain. As if that could really happen.

One week ago, Roman rang me up to ask me to go away with him. Seems he was attending a sort of symposium for his profession, one held every year, but he'd missed the previous year's event and was adamant about going this time. It was being held clear across the country and would I go with him? My heart leapt at the thought, and after a few properly demure words about what people might think, he said "Forget all that nonsense, Valerie." And so I agreed to go with him.

I won't go into detail about the symposium itself, for I didn't attend much of it myself, owing to the fact that much of it is closed to the public, and despite my being there with Roman it remained so. I spent some happy hours in my hotel suite and at a theater right down the street, and when it was over we boarded our train for the long trip back.

There was a long delay at the station—I never did find out why—but we were finally on our way, dinner served very late, but sometimes these inconveniences can't be avoided. It was quite dark when we'd finished and then retired to a small sitting area at one end of the dining car. The train cars are old, at least thirty years or more, but very well maintained and still opulent, a feast for the eyes from the previous century. Full of good food and drink and with both the not-unpleasant aroma of the men's cigars—I learned to like the smell of Father's smokes long ago—and the slight swaying of the train, I found myself comfortably sleepy as we sat.

There was Roman and myself, a teacher from the south on holiday, two older ladies of a poorer sort, and, of all things, a politician, Mr. Daniel Clowers, and his daughter Laura. I was a bit vague on exactly what Mr. Clowers' political position was in the government, and his name not being familiar to me, I assumed he was being truthful with us. Laura Clowers is, oh, most likely sixteen or so, maybe a bit older, plain but not homely, and dressed fashionably for girls her age. She was distant throughout dinner and later, and

I guessed she was bored with her father's puffery and pronouncements. Frankly, I wasn't too fond of them myself. The man spoke well, but at length and never seemed to say much of anything once he was through. A typical politician. The government is full of them.

It was all I could do to keep my eyes open while the men conversed. Roman was being polite, I could tell, as Clowers asked a series of questions about "just what it is" that Roman does exactly. I tried to listen, but my body was feeling the weight of the day's long hours and, forgive me, I began to drift off to sleep. The politician's droning voice helped in that as he, if memory serves, kept circling back around to what appeared to be the same question though worded differently each time. He was concerned, apparently, over how the "universe at-large," i.e. God, I suppose, justifies the "system" that Roman works within.

A quick note of reminder: Roman Janus is, well, a hunter of ghosts. There was a time when I was a firm non-believer in such things, but recently I have seen things that I cannot explain in earthly terms and what I've experienced in the past few hours…let me try to get on to that.

The talk was devolving into a lot of verbal sparring, not violently, mind you, but much back-and-forth with Mr. Clowers pressing his issue and Roman, bless him, smiling softly and holding his own, comfortable in his skin and his profession and having none of it. It was becoming rather dreary, that is until Laura abruptly left.

She had said little to nothing the entire evening, fending off her father's weak attempts to draw her into the conversation with a curt nod or a frown or even just turning her head away. I thought I saw some interest in the topic underneath the surface, but just as soon as I did it would melt away. I chalked it up to her young age and thoughts of boys or dresses or what have you. My own youth feels a million miles away, so what do I know of what today's young people think? Regardless, Laura was elsewhere, and if I didn't miss the mark by much, a trifle testy beyond it all. Then, she rose in the middle of one of her father's latest sallies against Roman's defenses and walked away. Just like that.

The teacher frowned at it, the old ladies *tsk*'d their disdain, and Mr. Clowers narrowed his eyes and shrugged his shoulders before dismissing Laura's departure and returning to his speech as if it never happened. How did I feel? Past the rudeness of her leaving in that fashion, I felt inexplicably sad for her.

Some minutes later, Roman held up his hand in the middle of the politician's questioning and uttered a single word: "Hold."

Roman has changed in some ways over the several months. He had disappeared for a year and we thought him murdered—which is entirely another story—but upon his reemergence he seemed to possess some new inner composure. Hard to describe exactly, but while he was the Roman Janus I knew of old, he was also a new man. One thing, though, that had not changed was his habit of appearing to look off into a distance that none of us around him could spy, as if he saw something far off that piqued his interest and he would like to see better. If anything, the habit intensified after he returned and at that moment in the railcar that look manifested like no other time I'd witnessed before.

"What are you doing, sir?" Mr. Clowers asked him. It sounded absurd to me, though of course it was what anyone might've said at the moment. The difference is in knowing Roman and his habits. But, I must admit, it gave me a fright that time. It wasn't that usual sort of lazy gaze of his, a spotting of something on the horizon that may or may not have merit, but a focused look of alarm, of great concern. With that and his single word he silenced the room and everyone in it. We all looked to him and as if by the combined effort of our very minds he rose from his couch and turned slowly in place, tracking something none of us could see.

"Valerie, forgive me," he said simply, and strode off toward the dining area without another word.

I, of course, followed. The dining area was still being cleared of the last dishes and cups and glasses and Roman wove his way in and around the quiet activity. The staff paid little attention to him, but as he approached the door on the far end of the car a colored conductor appeared by his side and spoke to him. Roman paused and turned to the man, a short, stocky representative of his kind, immaculate in his uniform and cap. He maintained the proper distance from Roman, but questioned him, no doubt as to whether he could help. Roman shook his head, smiled, and gestured toward the door as he turned to move through it. The conductor followed.

Continuing on my way, I could barely see Roman then for the conductor between us. I grew annoyed at the man's interference and was about to question his purpose in following Roman, but bit back on calling out to him. At the moment, I didn't feel like explaining my own part in the parade, and my curiosity over Roman's own purposes overwhelmed all else.

Our train-within-a-train made its way into the next car, a more formal lounge bigger than the one we'd just left. A few passengers occupied it, sitting at the bar or reclining in chairs at tables, but for the most part uninterested in our passage. Beyond the conductor ahead of me I saw Roman stop and look over the bar, but then continue on his way again. After passing through the vestibule, we entered into a car full of sleeping berths, private areas accessible by lockable doors. Roman slowed his pace through the car, treading his way down the passageway outside the berths. I saw his head turn from time to time to glance at them, as if he were looking or *listening* for something. The conductor did not molest him; perhaps he was as entranced as I in the strange production, though I had the benefit of knowing Roman's odd habits in advance.

The next car was also a sleeper, and in fact the one which held our own berths, mine and Roman's, save at the far end of it. Roman paused and finally stopped altogether in front of the second door from the vestibule. The conductor approached him and asked him what if anything was wrong. Roman held up one hand to him; not rudely, exactly, but simply to tell him to wait a moment, I would guess. I came up from behind the conductor and Roman only glanced at me before returning his attention to the door. He reached out and knocked on it, but received no reply. The conductor spoke again, I couldn't make out his words clearly that time, for his voice was low and tended to blend in with the general rumbling of the train around us. Roman shook his head but did not avert his eyes from the door. They had a serious cast to them, one that produced a note of concern in me.

A voice spoke unexpectedly behind me, causing me to jump slightly. "Why, that's my daughter's berth, sir," it said. I wheeled around angrily to face our friend the politician, Mr. Daniel Clowers.

Roman only nodded matter-of-factly. The conductor turned around to stare first at me and then Mr. Clowers. I didn't care for the scrutinizing look in his eyes, but I suppose it was his job to know what was going on aboard the train. He opened his mouth to speak, but Roman spoke over him, asking the politician if he would please see if his daughter was in and could talk with him for a moment. Clowers cleared his throat, a nervous affectation I noted in him from our earlier time in the sitting area, and frowned. "An unusual request," he pronounced, and I could see him beginning to puff up, the imminent arrival of the true politician within him. Roman shook his head to derail his obvious train of thought.

"I don't ask lightly, Mr. Clowers," he told the man, "but it may be a matter of some urgency."

This appeared to alarm him, as well as it should have, I suppose, but to his credit he swallowed it and quickly recovered, no doubt also due to his political abilities. Clowers stepped forward to shoulder the conductor aside and centered himself on the door to his daughter's berth. Roman allowed him the dominant position but hung close to the man's side as Clowers raised his hand, and set his knuckles to the door, once, twice, and called out to his child.

I leaned closer myself, but heard no reply, nor any other sound on the other side. The politician called out again, but with a change in tone. Now it was softer, perhaps to reassure Laura that nothing was wrong. I watched Roman throughout, expecting him to grow more apprehensive, but I should have known he'd maintain his composure. He turned to Clowers and spoke to him again.

"I'm sorry to persist in this, sir, but I must see her, speak to her."

Clowers raised his knuckles again to knock. The conductor stirred; I'd forgotten he was even there, so silently did he stand beside our little group. He said something in his low voice, but again I didn't quite hear what it was. Roman looked to him and shook his head, thanking him but telling him it wasn't necessary *yet*. It was then I saw the conductor's eyes dart from Roman to the politician and to me. I stared back, wondering why he was there at all.

Knocking anew, Clowers put more force into his voice as he pronounced his daughter's name, not as a question but as a firm statement. It was clear what he meant: *open this door immediately*. Roman's shoulders twisted slightly and I saw that he was growing restless at the delay…at the moment I couldn't guess what he was so concerned about. Finally, the door swung open and Clowers, amazingly, looked to Roman, who bowed his head in silent appreciation and made his way through the open portal to the room beyond. This was the special presence of Roman Janus at work, his quiet command of a room and of a situation.

The politician entered on Roman's heels. My own concern for the girl overtook me and I moved to approach the open doorway, but found the conductor suddenly in my path. There was a slight impact and I shifted back, surprised. The man turned his dark face to me and nodded, saying, "Pardon me, ma'am. Are you with the gentlemen?"

I was annoyed at first, but reason calmed me and inwardly I realized it might look odd for me to expect to enter the room. Feeling that I owed the conductor no explanation, I merely took another step or two backward until I came to rest with a window at my back, but still with a view into the cabin. In it I saw Roman addressing the girl with her father at his side, both men gazing down at her as she sat on her bed, looking up at them with innocent eyes. I strained my ears to hear what was being said, and to my amazement the conductor stepped out of my way to allow me to inch a bit closer.

"Father—what is it?" I heard Laura ask, her eyes on Clowers alone. I felt as if she were purposely avoiding Roman's gaze as he studied her room with his own eyes.

"Our friend the sergeant," replied her father, "well, I'm not sure, but he—"

"Pardon me for asking, Miss Clowers," Roman said, "but what have you been doing since leaving us?"

The girl's cheeks reddened. I could see she was still fully clothed, though having removed her shoes. I could see nothing from my vantage point that she might be hiding—cigarettes? Alcohol? Something stronger? I still wasn't sure what Roman was on about, and why he felt something was amiss with her. The politician dropped his shoulders in exasperation and turned to Roman as if to ask why he'd barged into his daughter's berth to disturb her.

Roman tried to affix a smile to face. "Miss Clowers, I am very sorry and hope you'll forgive me. I grew concerned about you after you left us. Is there anything you'd like to tell me—tell your father, of course?"

Laura assured them that nothing was wrong, that she was simply tired and was preparing for bed. Roman bowed slightly to her and swung his arm around to indicate the door to Mr. Clowers. The man shook his head and chuckled, then exited first, bidding his daughter pleasant dreams. Roman followed, but at the threshold abruptly swung back around to the girl, took one long step into the room and snatched at her bed covers with a hand.

Pulling the blankets aside with one swift movement, he revealed something there on the bed, hidden beneath them.

Laura gave a little shriek of surprise. Clowers barked Roman's name. I felt the conductor stiffen at my side as I moved back to see what had been revealed: a Ouija board.

Roman cocked one hand upon his hip while stroking his chin with his other. Laura stared at the board but then turned her head from it, silently refusing to look up at Roman. Clowers sputtered his daughter's name, then Roman's again, obviously flummoxed by the incident.

"Miss Clowers," Roman began, his voice kind, but also stern in a way, "I felt it was something like this." He indicated the board. "I cannot recommend it. I cannot recommend it in the very strongest terms. The talking board is not a toy or a game. It is a *tool*, and not one to be used blithely."

The girl found her voice, but only slightly, to begin to form a rebuttal, but her father interjected. "Laura—you know how I feel about this!"

I will never forget the venom in the girl's voice when she swung around to her father and said: "You're only concerned with your *career*."

Roman, bless him, took a step between the two and laid one hand on the politician's shoulder. "I feel as if a note of warning is all that's needed here, Clowers. Your daughter's a very smart and clever girl. I think she'll realize what I'm telling her comes from my heart, and from my experience." He looked back at Laura. "Miss Clowers—Laura—please, I urge you to pack the board up and never use it again. I've seen people much older and wiser than you misuse it and regret their actions for the rest of their lives."

The words hung there in the little cabin. The girl looked up at Roman finally, slowly nodded to him, and reached out to pick up the board and fold it closed.

"Thank you," Roman told her plainly. "To continue to use the talking board would be the same as opening your door here for anyone at all, any stranger, to walk right in as if they had an engraved invitation."

He looked up just then as he indicated the doorway to see me standing there. Our eyes met and he offered me a strange, sad smile.

Clowers shuffled out of the room telling his daughter they'd talk about it in the morning. Roman clapped him on the back in reassurance and bade him a good night. He then looked at the conductor and assured the man that everything was all right as he gathered me up and we looked down the passageway toward our own rooms. As I turned to go, something inside prompted me to look back at Laura Clowers as she began to shut her door.

"I'm here if you'd like to talk about anything, Laura," I told her in earnest. As I sit her in my own room writing this out for you, dear diary, I can still see the girl's cold gaze and curt shake of her head as she shut and latched the door.

I'm heading to bed now myself. Roman seemed uninterested in saying anything about the incident before he retired to his room, and all this writing has exhausted any remaining energy left in me.

Valerie

My love,

All I can think about is you. My father had no right to come looking for me and take me away from you, but I guess he's used to getting his way. He said no one knows about it and no one will ever know about it. He also said some very cruel things to you, and I'm very sorry about that. I won't say he doesn't mean them because I know he does.

We're on the train and I'm barely speaking to him. Tonight he embarrassed me again, not as much as when he took me away on this trip, but nearly as much and he'll be lucky if I ever speak to him again after this.

He caught me with my board *in my own room*. It's such a stupid, silly thing and the worst of it is he did it in front of other people. He made friends with a man here on the train, a military man of some kind who thinks he knows all about spirits and gets *rid of them* for people. He and my father nearly broke the door of my room down when the man—well, I'm sure my father put him up to it, but the man acted like he *knew* I had the board. It's all so silly I could scream. This man made as if *he* found me and then gave me a warning about what I was doing, that I'd *regret* it or some stupid thing. And then the stupid cow of a woman that's with him tried to make doeeyes at me as if she were my friend!

If I can, I'm going to use the board every chance I get from now on.

I just tried to sleep some, because I feel *so tired*, but had a very strange dream. It does no good to sit here and do nothing, so I want to tell you about it.

I was somewhere else other than on this train and there were clouds all around me. I felt the ground moving below me as if I was on the train but I couldn't see it anywhere. There was a rumbly sound off in the distance that at first I thought might be the train, but after a bit it sounded more like a horse's hoof beats. I was moving, I think, like I said, so I wasn't sure if the sounds were coming at me or along with me.

Then suddenly there was a girl in front of me. She looked to be about my age, very pretty—please don't be jealous—and she looked right at me. I'm not sure how she was dressed because the clouds all around us made her clothes hard to see, but very quickly, only for a moment, I thought she might be naked. Anyway, I couldn't move so I couldn't approach her and she didn't seem to be approaching me so we just stood there and looked at each other. Then, she opened her mouth and looked like she was going to say something...but she couldn't. Or didn't. I'm not sure which. But then the frightening thing happened: she burst into *flames*.

I awoke at that moment to find myself on this wretched train and you not there beside me. I love you so much it hurts.

I will slip this into the mail as soon as I can, maybe at the next stop if my father even lets me out of his sight.

Laura

Assistant Conductor - Day Log
June 9

The train left the station four hours past our scheduled departure time due to the late arrival of foodstuffs from Milner's Produce. I recommend the company consider a change in delivery service. The passengers remained patient for the most part, but three complaints were logged with my conductors. We got under way at 7:34 and dinner was served at 8:10; roast beef, glazed carrots, asparagus, rice pilaf, baked Alaska.

Most diners retired to the lounge following the meal, but some few chose the side lounge for drinks and cigars. This group included Mr. D. Clowers, a politician of some note, and his young daughter. I will be reminding the dining staff to be more attentive to his requests, owing to his many changes throughout the meal.

Clean-up in the dining car proceeded without delay with only one incident to report.

Passenger R. Janus became disturbed during after-dinner drinks and conversation, and I approached him to determine if I could render any assistance. The man declined my offer, but asked that my help be available should it become necessary, though he could not inform me of the nature of the problem. Due to his unusual behavior and reluctance to provide details of what troubled him, I followed Mr. Janus as he left the dining car and lounge. From there he entered the adjacent sleeping car, but without satisfaction, and so entered the next. At this time I was unaware other persons in his party had begun to follow him and myself.

Upon entering the next sleeping car, Mr. Janus approached passenger L. Clowers' berth, where he received no response to his knock. I chose to remind him of company policies involving the privacy of guests, but at that moment Mr. Clowers made his appearance and insisted his daughter open her door. Words were exchanged between the parties and when I heard their conversation, which involved a family dispute, determined no violence would occur, nor any rule or policy was being broken. Another passenger, Mrs. V.

Havelock-Mayer, also arrived at the disturbance, but I could see she was not overly involved.

The group then dispersed to their own individual rooms without further incident. Mr. Clowers ordered a nightcap sent to his berth. All other guests onboard remained quiet with no more such events occurring for the remainder of the evening.

June 10

Dear Diary,

I have willed my hands to stop trembling long enough for me to write this. At least I believe I have succeeded in that, but we'll see.

The morning sun is just about to rise, but the dark clouds surrounding it may keep it muted today. The train moves along to our destination, but all I can think about is the last two hours. They have shaken me something terrible. I have seen something...I shouldn't be surprised by this! What I experienced almost a year ago in that courtroom should have prepared me for what I saw—here on this train! But Roman saw it, too, and because of that I know I am not going mad. It only feels like I am.

Let me try to think. It's hard, very hard...

All right. How did it begin? I went to my bed feeling tired, but once I lay down I couldn't stop thinking about Laura Clowers. About her face when she looked out of her cabin at us departing. I sensed how she felt about the discovery, and about her father. She blamed it all on her father. They have a problem, something that is holding them apart, and I know all too well what that feels like. I know what is to be angry at a father.

I lay there for what seemed like hours, my mind busy over the problem and, knowing that Roman was only in the next room to mine, wondered if he was sleeping or if he, too, wondered about the girl. I saw it in him, or at least I think I saw it, his concern over her welfare with that Ouija board—which are damnably stupid things. Why do some people put such stock in them? I thought the Spiritualist movement to be done and over, a lark we as a society finally cast off in the end as a pointless parlor game. And the boards with it. Maybe I'm the wrong person to believe that, seeing as what I saw nearly a year ago, but I can't reconcile the two things for some reason.

Back to Laura.

After finally only drowsing—trains usually lull me to sleep!—I got up, put on my dressing gown and looked for the book I'd started before we left on the trip. It was just then that I thought I heard a door open somewhere close, and I thought it might be Roman's. I then felt drawn to look out into the corridor, and so I did, but saw nothing but the dark passage with its lights low and the slight shaking from the train's progress...

Then I saw it.

I'm compelled at this moment to say *him* rather than *it*, but nothing since I saw the figure truly leads me to believe it was human, or deserving of the label "human." It was all dark and...

Stepping out into the passageway, I could see it at the end of it, near the door to the outside deck between our car and the next. At first it was formless, like a mist, or simply a dark smudge in the air, as if someone had drubbed dark grey, almost black paint on a pane of glass and left in the corridor. But as I watched, it *quivered* and seemed to grow. I blinked, hardly believing my eyes, and then it was a man.

Yes, I've written the word, Dear One, but I put little stock in it. I only use it here to give some grounding to my thoughts, a foundation on which to build what I'm trying to say, to explain. I blinked my eyes to clear them and the smudge was suddenly man-shaped. As tall as an adult and radiating maleness. Even now I can feel the sensation, as if being in the presence of a wholly male, wholly...*dominant* persona. I recovered from the sensation quickly—I grew up with such a man around me—and told myself I'd only imagined the formless, shapeless dark spot previously. This was another passenger, surely, having trouble sleeping or wandered into the wrong car, or...

I saw its feet were not touching the floor.

My eyes left the patch of wooden boards I could see underneath its feet, or what I perceived as its feet, and traveled up its length to its torso and then to its head, expecting to see a face or simply eyes staring at me. None could be discerned in the place where they should have been. Thank God for that. I simply couldn't have stood for the idea of it *looking* at me. As it was, my skin crawled in the thing's presence, a million beetles covering me from head to toe. Even my eyes itched, but I could not raise a hand to rub at them. I was transfixed by the vision before me.

In an instant, the thought of putting my hand to my face brought me to notice something about the figure: Its own hands were *twitching*. Why? In that moment, I didn't know, couldn't fathom it, but when the hands began to slap at the figure's thighs I realized in horror what would come next.

The hands twitched again and *lengthened*, stretching into new shapes, long and slender extensions of the original members. I recognized them at once.

Pistols.

Diary, as you well know, I have been around guns and men with guns my entire life. My brothers, my father, his soldiers, and my husband; all gun owners and users. I am not frightened of guns, nor men with guns, but the sight of the specter standing in the corridor on this train brandishing what appeared to be pistols at the ends of its arms filled me with a dread I cannot name. I should have turned away, back into my room, but I couldn't. I couldn't will my body to do it.

The low lights in the passage flickered just then, and grew softer. I felt cold, oh so *cold*! Colder than anything I'd ever felt before, as if every ounce of heat was leaving my body, from my extremities to my very core, and then to...

Ah. I see it now. The thing drew the light, the heat from all around it to itself. Stole it. Stole it from *me*, also.

The next ticks of the clock were amorphous to me, barely something I comprehend now, beyond the pull of the dark figure. Hands touched me, took me by my arms, my neck, and then covered my face, pressing over my mouth, my nose, down upon my eyes. Something told me to scream, but as far as I know I didn't. My feet...left the floor. I was being carried away...

Roman's face. That's what I remember then, coming up out of a haze, a fog, looming over me, but not frightening, not horrid. Not unwelcome. I said his name, lifted my head, and tried to pull him closer to me, still so very, very cold.

"Valerie," he said, concern in his strange eyes, "can you hear me?"

What an odd thing to ask, I thought immediately. Why would I be unable to hear? Why would that be his first question to me?

The thing! In the corridor! Just outside the room—for I could see I was back in my own room. Roman assured me the event had passed and I was safe. He would allow no harm to come to me.

But he was troubled, Dear Diary. So troubled. More so than what I saw in his face over the girl's Ouija board. He had been *shaken*. And I didn't care for the look of it upon him.

Regardless, he told me to try to sleep as he rose from his perch on the side of my bed and turned to leave the room. I asked him what had happened and where he was going, and he once again passed along his assurance that I was safe and that he was seeing to the safety of the entire train.

With that he was gone, and I fell into an uneasy sleep to wake a short time later from splinters of a dream, nervous and jittery, to begin to write it all down to you.

And I am still cold.

Valerie

Assistant Conductor - Day Log
June 10

The night-duty conductor informed me this morning of two incidents during his shift, both of which I have reported to the conductor. One, a small fire broke out in the galley in Car 6, but was put out
immediately after being discovered by a cook. It did not burn long
and no passengers in the adjoining Car 5 or Car 7 were aware of it.
Apparently food was left on a still-hot stove, but the cook swears he
turned the stove off as he normally does after dinner is over. Otherwise there was no good reason for the fire to have started.

Second, passengers in Car 7 noted both flickering lights in their
rooms and in the corridor outside their rooms, and a loss of heat
during the night. I am directing my people to check all light switch-
es and bulbs, as well as all heaters for failure. If this shows no evidence of faulty equipment or wiring, I will also put in an order for an
electrician once the train is back at the home station.

I am now beginning my rounds, including going over the day's
menus and other matters with my people. One stop will be to check
in with Mr. Clowers to see if all is well with his daughter after last
evening's incident.

CROSS-COUNTRY LTD - 10 JUNE

TO: MRS. DANIEL CLOWERS
WEYFORTH, THE CITY

EMILY

LAURA CAUSING DISTRESS AGAIN. WAS GOOD UN-
TIL LAST NIGHT, HAD BOARD OUT AGAIN. CALL DR
YAMOB IMMEDIATELY TO SCHEDULE APPT NEXT
WEEK. INSIST ON NEW REGIMEN. NO ARGUMENTS.
ALSO CALL SHOTTEN TO DRAW UP LETTER TO THAT
GIRL'S PARENTS. MUST STOP ALL CONTACT, AGAIN
NO ARGUMENTS. HOME IN THREE DAYS. CONVEN-
TION MEETING ON MONDAY, NOTHING IN MY WAY
GOING FORWARD.

DANIEL

Dear Diary,

I'm ducking into your pages to share with you a conversation I just had, one which I find alarming. Roman arrived not long after I woke this morning and was trying to decide if I wanted to eat something. Upon seeing him at my door, I sat him down and pounced on what I believed to be the single most important question of the moment:

"What was that thing?"

Roman, while generally circumspect with others, is generally open and honest with me. He stared me right in the face and said, "A spirit. And a rather malevolent one. In fact, one of the worst I've ever encountered—and I needn't tell *you* I've encountered quite a few."

I digested that, knowing full well what his answer would be, though perhaps not with as much emphasis as to its nature he gave. I then asked him what in the wide world it was doing on a *train*, of all things. Roman, God love him, looked at me as if I were a child, an innocent. It was something he hadn't done in a long while, owing to our more recent history together. It shamed me, embarrassed me.

"Valerie, these entities are not tied to one place," he explained. "Not always. The idea of a spirit manifesting only in a certain room or on the grounds of an estate, or even from a singular object, this is a matter of fancy, borne from fiction and fable, not reality. They are no more chained to one house, one room, one courtyard, one…doll, I guess, than you or me. Yes, some are prisoners of a sort, unable to move from a spot that somehow played a role in an important event in their past life, but I tell you that more often than not, those chains are of their own making."

Leave it to Roman to offer an explanation that would sound so matter-of-fact to him, so commonplace and obvious, but to the rest of us mere mortals merely incredible.

I proceeded to ask him about the intense feeling of cold, and the lights.

Taking my hand and patting it, he said, "Sometimes they want this. The light that is in all of us. And sometimes they can take it to make themselves stronger on this plane. To strengthen their ties to it."

"Why," I continued, "here and now?"

A cloud came into his eyes and his gaze lost some of its intensity. He said nothing, offered no answer. For a long moment he just looked at me, as if to impart something without words—words he disliked the taste of.

It dawned on me all at once. "Oh, no," I told him, and bit my lip in consternation and unbelief. "You can't mean..."

"Yes," was his answer. And I hated him a little bit for it, and told him I couldn't comprehend it.

"I need to speak to Laura Clowers as soon as possible," he said, rising from his chair. "I must stop her from using the board again. I warned her, and now here is the result of her mischief: This dark thing onboard, you in danger, and..."

I insisted that even if it had come onto the train once, it didn't mean it would continue to do so. Perhaps it was a fluke, a once-done happenstance that would surely not continue with such a man as Roman Janus on the same train, but I suddenly remembered what the spirit was trying to do—trying to *manifest*.

I tried to tell him about the pistols.

"Pistols?" he inquired, obviously unaware of it. "If true, it makes things even more urgent." He paused, chewing on something, which was very unlike him. Looking into his eyes again, I saw a degree of reluctance in them that made me ill at ease, an uncanny amount of holding back for Roman Janus. I asked, no, implored him to tell me what he wasn't saying about the encounter.

"I...stopped it," Roman explained, "but only just barely. And that is all I care to say about it at this time, Valerie. Now, will you come with me to the Clowers? I saw how you were with the girl, and she with you. I may need your help."

Now, I ask you, Dear One; how could I refuse an invitation like that?

Valerie

Speech Notes (Excerpt) – Daniel Clowers

"...we stand at the doorway to yet another of those times in history when more than one path lies before us. And I must stress to you all that a misstep at this juncture could be disastrous. At too many such divergence points in the past have we chosen unwisely and opened ourselves to misery and hardship, when what we should be doing is counting our blessings, taking stock in our larders, and trusting in the tried and true path that has always carried us through to prosperity and stability.

What am I trying to say, you ask? Just this, my friends: the unknown is all around us, beckoning to us with its siren's call, seductive and full of promise—but it is only empty promise it offers, I can assure you. You may like what it has to say, what rewards it seems to hold, but—and you'll forgive me a dip into the Good Book—the Devil's words are sweet.

Am I saying my opponent is the Devil? Hardly. I can assure you he does not sport a tail and cloven hooves (wait for laughter). No, what I am saying to you today is that he is an unknown quantity, a path seemingly full of promise, but in truth not a stable one. We know little about him, yet you know all the important details of my life, my family, my work. I am an open book! Read from my pages and you will find a life similar to yours, and one you can wholly relate to. I am stable and secure; there are no surprises with me, my friends. What you see here before you today is what you will receive once the votes are submitted and tallied. And you will thank me when we turn to step back onto that tried and true path...together.

I humbly thank you for your consideration. My wife and my daughter thank you, too..."

Dear Diary,

Two things have happened.

One, the train has stopped. Two, I have decided to carry you with me at all times.

The first thing was surprising, not because we have never stopped—we have at times—but because we passengers have been told it's something of an emergency. It seems a fire broke out in a kitchen last night, and while the chief conductor says that such events are not entirely unusual, the fact that he and his staff cannot determine the source and the reason for the fire is. I suppose there's some concern over faulty electrical wiring, or even incompetence among the cooks, but if the latter surely they could have kept going to our destination without pausing for an indeterminate length of time while what appears to be an investigation proceeds.

Then again, what I don't know of the workings of trains, though I've been on a few in my time, would fill a few books. Still, I shouldn't be flippant about it; I'm glad they are taking it seriously.

Mr. Daniel Clowers, our resident politician, is also taking it seriously, to the point of lividity. He has taken his complaints over the matter to the highest authority onboard, and even from what little I know of him, most likely beyond.

Laura Clowers is nowhere to be seen.

The second point I made stems from a flash of insight I had after ending my last missive to you: I have become a chronicler.

To wit, Roman has a curious habit and history of never writing anything down about his "adventures" or "cases." He leaves that to those who hire or engage him, incredibly. It never ceases to amaze me how many people have bowed to his odd wishes and have recorded the details of the goings-on they experienced while the man himself investigated their problems, but, alas, here I am doing much the same thing and not realizing it until this morning. So, for expedience's sake, I have you along for the journey and at my fingertips as things happen.

Much has happened already, and if the events of the past hour or so are any indication, much is left to further transpire. And with me in the middle of it.

Once we were told that the train was being stopped at a depot in a small town somewhere in the middle of nowhere and that no timetable was being set for our departure—or so we're told—Roman turned to me and said, "No time like the present to talk to Laura Clowers."

I liked the tone in his voice at that moment, and the slight gleam in his eye. He was motivated and had something in his teeth to chew on. My own personal vision of our immediate future was a battle royale with the girl's father; given his mood over the stoppage, there was nothing he could be happy about being approached by a ghost-hunter to talk to him about his daughter and her Ouija board.

I could commend myself on my prescience, but it was surely a given considering the circumstances and the cast of characters.

"No, not now, sir," were Daniel Clowers exact words when Roman asked his permission to talk with Laura about her use of the board the night before. He seemed very unsteady and unfocused just then for a politician, but when he further explained he wasn't in a frame of mind for it and it would have to be later or not at all, Roman demonstrated just how very persuasive he can be when he wants.

"Last evening, when we were talking, you showed interest in my profession, though I could tell your true interest was scant. You're a talker, Mr. Clowers—that's *your* profession. But your very intelligent daughter, while seemingly disinterested in the conversation, was listening intently."

Clowers frowned very slightly, but invited Roman to continue.

"Laura has used the talking board, here on this train, last night, and in doing so I suspect has stirred up something I'm sure she never expected."

The politician isn't a stupid man, and while I could see he struggled with himself internally, most likely weighing what it could all mean to his career, I could see he was taking Roman seriously...or at least mostly seriously. He must have felt there was something in what Roman was telling him. He confirmed this by explaining that his own grandmother had dabbled in such things and as a boy it gave him pause—what an admission for a politician to make to perfect strangers.

"You may speak to her, sir," he said, his eyes dark, "but only briefly. Perhaps *you* can get through to her on this matter, where I have been…unable."

Roman assured him that my presence might help keep Laura in a more reasonable frame of mind; woman-to-woman, so to speak. At first I took it as simple pragmatism on Roman's part, not fully seeing what he apparently had already divined. More on that in a bit. We three then made our way to Laura Clowers' room and confronted her.

As I assumed, her hackles rose immediately. Before Roman or her father had said much of anything at all, she fired away at them.

"Are you going to take it away from me?" she said in an indignant tone, her eyes cold fire. Interestingly enough, no one had even mentioned the Ouija board yet. Roman shook his head and told her in a calm, reassuring voice that only her father could do that.

"And so I am," Clowers informed her, *his* voice leaving nothing ambiguous.

Laura looked at the three of us in rapid succession, and I saw a caged animal in her eyes then. I started to speak, trying to think of something that would cut through her defenses, make her see the importance in it, but she stood up suddenly and reared back, her gaze going to a spot in the room where I guessed the board was hidden.

Roman stood up and reached out his hand to touch her arm, and Laura flinched violently from it. I swear even the skin on her arm spasmed, too. Things fell into place in my mind, and dismissing a quick thought that perhaps she'd been beaten by her father in the past, I realized, very clearly, that she was a sapphist.

"Laura," Roman said, "let me see your eyes."

The girl narrowed said orbs and shot daggers at him. "I'm not a *cocaine addict*, if that's what you mean!"

Clowers shouted, "Laura! Good God!" and the entire conversation was then lost to chaos. Whatever good intentions Roman had, whatever mission he was on exactly, crumbled right then and there.

He took a step back, first dropping his arms to his sides, then flooding them across his chest. My heart leapt to him in his defeat.

"Mr. Clowers," he said to the politician, "I'm sorry I must insist on this point, but if you value your daughter's life—and if you feel she values it herself—take the talking board from here and destroy it. Or there will be true destruction on hand."

And with that he turned and left, leaving me standing there with father and daughter, neither of them in a mood to continue the conversation. I bid them a good day and hurried out, feeling entirely lost in the circumstances and completely blind as to what might come next.

Valerie

Oh, My Love,

I'm adrift and I don't know what to do. My life is crumbling before my eyes. *I do know I've got to get off this train and back to you!*
We've stopped, you see, in the middle of nowhere all because of a fire they say, some stupid little thing that doesn't mean a thing. If I didn't know better, I'd say my father had them stop the train just to cause me grief—my father! *He took the board away! He actually took it away!* And do you know why, past his being all together cruel and dull? That man I told you about before, the spirit-man? *He* told my father to take it away from me. I'm at wit's end. I can't believe it. He just walked right up to my father and told him to do it and the idiot my father is, he did it. And that man had to gall to *touch me!*
Don't even have me start about that woman who's with the man—she goes along with everything he says, no matter what. Stands there and smiles at him with her moon eyes—the cow!—I think they're probably lovers! It makes me sick to look at them!
And speaking of being sick, I don't feel well. I feel ill sometimes, like I'm burning up, but then it goes away and I feel cool and... dead. Dead inside.
If only I could feel your arms around me, Cleo! I know I'd feel better.
Why is everyone against me? Why do they constantly try to make my life miserable? I want to go home, but...home isn't right. That's why I left, isn't it? My father said—*he's not my father! I hate him! Charlie treated me better until he got mean and then I had to leave him, too! I have no father! I don't want a father! I want to go home! I never want to see home again! I don't have a home! I want to burn down the world!*

What did I just write? I didn't mean—why?

Cleo, I'm scared.

CROSS-COUNTRY LTD - 10 JUNE

TO: MRS. DANIEL CLOWERS
WEYFORTH, THE CITY

EMILY

LAURA COMPLETELY OUT OF CONTROL. TOOK THE
BOARD AWAY AND NOT SPEAKING TO ME AT ALL.
WE ARE STOPPED FOR SOME REASON. NO SIGN OF
MOVEMENT. UTTERLY UNACCEPTABLE. AM TAK-
ING MY GRIEVANCE TO ENGINEER, CONDUCTOR,
EVERYONE AND ANYONE. I NEED TO RETURN WITH
LAURA WITHOUT FURTHER DELAY. BE READY.

DANIEL

Assistant Conductor - Day Log
June 10

We have been unable to find the cause of the fire. My people went over the stove from top to bottom, but could see no reason for a fire to break out. One of my people even suggested we try to duplicate the event to see how it might have happened, but that proved nothing as we could not get a fire to start without the proper steps in starting the stove for regular cooking.

Strangely, though, at one point during the examination one of the cooks, Manfred Hunt, received a good burn on his left arm near the wrist. He saw no flame before it happened, or so he says, but another person near him saw him jump up and yell from pain, and when they looked he had not only a burn on his arm but all that goes with it. It looked as if somehow flames jumped onto his arm from somewhere, burnt him, and then went out.

As for the heaters, again we can find nothing wrong with them or their wiring. Every test we have made with them shows they work well and with no problems. I have suggested we can use them, but they must be checked every half-hour for faults.

As to the stove, we will not use it, but instead use another stove on board in its place until we can have it removed at some time in the near future.

I have also received complaints from several passengers over our delay in starting back on our way. The strongest such complaints have come from Mr. Clowers. One thing I feel I must note about the gentleman is that one of my staff overheard loud words or an argument between him and Mr. Janus earlier. This happened in the room of Mr. Clowers daughter. It did not go on for long, but my man told me that Mr. Janus left the room hurriedly and in sour humor, and his companion, Mrs. Havelock-Mayer, left not a moment later.

I do not believe strong spirits were involved in the matter, owing to the time of day it happened, but I will speak to the bartender to see if this is actually the case.

Now, I am heading to give my recommendation for us to get under way again to the conductor and the engineer, though I still have misgivings about all these incidents.

Dear Diary,

For the rest of the day I felt a growing sense of apprehension and looming consequence, wondering whether the apparition would appear again, and if so, where and when, not to mention if it would be even worse. I needn't have wondered; everything became all too clear all too soon.

Shortly past 1:00 in the afternoon we were told the train was ready to leave again, and within thirty minutes it did indeed leave the small town in which it had been dallying. We were also told that at the very next normal stop on our journey we would be taking on some new appliances and equipment, as well as an electrician, and that these additions might cause yet another delay. In the meantime, we were welcomed to arrange alternate modes of travel if we wished—with an accompanying refund of part of our fare.

I sought out Roman, feeling certain he wouldn't abandon the train no matter what the delays, and when he saw me he quickly assured me that was the case. He was prepared to see it through, whatever "it" was.

We sat down to talk in the dining car and he immediately spied you, Dear One. I opened my mouth to offer an explanation, but he lightly tapped my hand with his fingertips and gave me a slight smile and a nod. Through those I knew he both understood and encouraged my chronicling, as it were.

"What should we expect?" I asked him, perhaps with a bit more strain in my voice than I'd intended. Roman frowned and leaned toward me over the table. "'We' should not expect anything, Valerie," he said gravely. "This is my profession; not yours."

There was no malice in his voice, no condescension, no disrespect; that's not the kind of man he is. But, it still rankled and I told him so, protesting I was already a part of it and I wanted to see it through. A wall went up within him; I saw it immediately, and though I disliked the sound of it and the implication, I asked him to humor me.

"I'm worried about Laura," I explained truthfully. "I'm worried about *you*. I'm worried about the passengers on this train. If I can do something, anything to help, then that's what I want to do."

Roman appraised me with a look I interpreted as "You've come a long way, Valerie," but I dismissed it and continued on, saying how I'd felt since my encounter last night and how I found that sleeping, reading, eating, all the normal things people do on a train were hollow and empty to me. All I could think about was that man—*that spirit.*

Before I could say more, the colored conductor from yesterday came by our table and stopped to say, "Good afternoon, ma'am, sir. Are you folks glad to be moving again?" Roman told him we were, and I merely nodded to the man, who from his uniform seemed to be the *assistant* conductor. Roman then asked him his name, to which he replied, "Butters, sir," and tipped his hat as he took a step past us to continue on his way. Just as soon as he'd taken the step, though, he paused and reversed himself.

"Sir," he addressed Roman, "I believe I owe you an apology." The man then proceeded to explain that he'd been referring to my companion as "Mr." all along, but somehow realized or discovered Roman was a "military person." Once it was made clear that the correct title was "Sgt.," the conductor tipped his hat again and said the most astonishing thing.

"I'm also to understand, and I hope you will pardon me, Sgt., that you are what some persons I know might call a 'hoodoo man'."

Frankly, I was nearly dumbfounded and arranged words to remonstrate the man for his rudeness, but Roman caught my eye and shook his head with a smile. "Yes, that's right, Mr. Butters—and, Valerie; I've been called much worse."

The conductor seemed embarrassed and apologized again, further noting that his, as he said at first "granny" and then corrected to "great-grandmother," was the kind of person who'd "get along fine" with such a gentleman as Roman. This sparked, of all things, a conversation between the two men, and before I knew it I was drifting away, apart from the talk and everything else around me. This went on until Roman's voice cut into my reverie calling out my name. When I acknowledged him, he suggested he was putting me to sleep, as I must be more tired than I'd thought, and why didn't I go lie down for a bit?

The conductor, obviously sensing he'd monopolized Roman, excused himself. Roman called after him, reminding the man he'd come to see him in a few hours to ask a few questions.

"What could you possibly ask of him?" I inquired, honestly intrigued by the arrangement. Apparently I'd missed more than most of their conversation, because Roman pointed out that the conductor had worked on the train for more than twenty years and would most likely know intimate details of its history, etc.

Well, Dear One, it was all important to Roman, though it wasn't clear to me what bearing it had on our situation, and I didn't care to argue the point. Though I wanted to press him about the odd reluctance he had to tell me why he seemed shaken after the encounter with the spirit, he escorted me back to my room, and quite alone in it I lay down to try to sleep, exhausted, confused, and not a little bit still apprehensive of what was to come.

To my surprise, sleep actually came to me. In fact, I nodded off almost immediately, and when I awoke I wasn't sure where I was or *when* it was. My sense of location and time were askew, and to my further surprise my watch had stopped sometime soon after I fell asleep. I also dreamed—oh, did I dream.

All I could recall upon waking were short bursts of scenes and sensations. I remembered a fire, and being extremely cold, an adventurous feeling as I jumped from one point to another, and the taste of exotic foods—and all the while someone near me. A man. And, I'm certain, not Roman.

Getting up and adjusting myself to look at least somewhat presentable, I left my room to knock softly on Roman's door. Receiving no response, I listened for a moment but all I heard was the clack-clack and tik-tik of the train in movement. Assuming he wasn't just sleeping, I left to make my way to the dining car, feeling ravenous and hoping it wasn't too late to grab a bit to eat.

The air all around me felt heavy with portent, and as I reached out to open the door to the dining car, the memory of the feeling of dread from before came rushing back to take my breath away. Trying to dispel it from my thoughts, I turned the door handle and stepped through the doorway… to find Roman standing a few yards away, his back to me, his body tensed as if to spring like a tiger.

Immediately I noticed someone lying on the floor near his feet, practically under one of the dining tables—and then I noticed another just a few feet away from the first. The people were unconscious, their eyes closed like they were sleeping. I couldn't understand it. Roman, without turning, yelled out my name, and then:

"*Get back!*"

He shifted just then, moving his shoulders and torso a mere few inches to one side and allowing me a view of what was in front of him. It was to ram home his point, I'm sure of it, and when I saw what it was, it was all I could do not to fly from the dining car right there and then.

A human form stood about ten feet from Roman, facing him. Tall and wearing a broad-brimmed hat, all dark as if in shadow, despite the lights burning at each dining table in the car. The figure seemed to *draw in the light* and turn it into darkness. I could see no face, or at least not at first. Staring hard at the head of the figure, and then looking just to the side of it and then back again, I thought I could just glimpse features—and they were devilish. I can think of no other word for them.

I knew without a shadow of doubt—I don't say it to make light of the situation—that it was the male spirit from the night before.

My sense of it was that Roman was blocking it, standing in its way or it would fly forward through the dining car to leap to the next—our own car. He was standing with his legs somewhat spread apart, but rock-steady, and his arms away from his sides, his palms turned toward the figure and nothing in them. The figure moved, ever so slightly, but not as a person moves, but more like smoke wafts through the air. It was all together unnerving.

Its one arm twitched and rose from its side and an index finger pointed at Roman—no, not just at him, but distinctly at his waist to one side. It wavered there in the air, pointing, and then reared back like a snake to jab the finger at him again. I could see it was trying to indicate something...

"No," Roman said, "I won't. Not unless I have to. This is my world, not yours—you don't get to call it."

His words were strange to me; what did he mean? What did the spirit want? Then, with cold dread I realized it wore guns on its own hips, as if in holsters held by a belt around its waist. A vision of its hands twitching at its sides the night before assailed me... it was like a gunfighter of the previous century, trying to get Roman to—what? To draw? Isn't that what they said? To draw his own weapons?

Good Lord, I thought; it was a showdown. A gunfight. The spirit was actually challenging Roman to a duel.

"Valerie," Roman called out to me, again not turning his head, his eyes locked on the smoky figure. "Protect...Laura. Go to her *now*. Stay *with* her. Whatever you do, do *not* leave her side."

Roman's hand moved to his side, to a place where if he wore a gunbelt the holster would sit. The spirit, apparently noticing it, wavered in the air like smoke being fanned.

"*Go!*"

I went. In fact, I ran.

Laura's room felt like it was across several train cars, not just the two—or was it three?—in reality. I tried not to think about what Roman was facing behind me, as well as what would truly be coming up from behind me if he failed. When I got to the Clowers' car, I hurried down the passageway and reached out for the handle of Laura's door, only to be stopped by a hand that reached out to grip my wrist with a sudden lurch. It was Daniel Clowers with a look of confusion mingled with anger on his face.

I told him I needed to see Laura immediately. He placed himself in front of the door. I said it was a matter of life and death. He made some sarcastic comment about me being Roman's surrogate in his campaign to come between him and his daughter. I wasn't sure where his anger arose from, exactly, but I didn't have time for it and tried to reach out again to grab the door handle. Clowers blocked me, rather brusquely.

So I punched him in the face.

Oh, my Dear Diary, perhaps you're shocked, but perhaps you've also forgotten I'd grown up with a military father and a clutch of brothers, and, well, fairly good looks and men who always seemed to think they were the only ones who could tame me.

I didn't quite knock him unconscious, pity, but the blow was quick and savage enough to stun him and he slumped against the door and fell away from it, moaning and holding his face in his hands. Wasting no time, I stepped over him and threw open Laura's door.

She lay still and unmoving on her bed and the room was engulfed in flames. Instinctively, whether from panic or fear, I reared back, throwing up one arm to block my face from the blaze and hoping my hair or my dress hadn't caught fire. Squinting through the conflagration I tried to see if the girl was insensate or perhaps at least semiconscious—the smoke by then should have overcome her, shouldn't it have? Laura looked completely unconscious, a prone form on the bed, looking for all the world like a small, sleeping princess.

It was at that moment I realized I felt no heat. My mind reeled… how could that be? The fire had spread throughout the room and was nearly licking the ceiling. Everything in the small area must be ablaze. I couldn't comprehend it. Where was the great, choking heat? And for that matter, why was the smoke not making cough and gasp for air?

And why wasn't everything within my sight burning?

I rubbed at my eyes, trying to clear them, and in a burst of courage I surely hadn't earned, I stretched out one arm and hand into the room—into the inferno. Nothing. Not heat, nothing. My sleeve did not catch fire, nor did the skin of my hand and arm blister and erupt from the tongues of fire that should have danced over it. I was not burning. The room was not burning. Most important of all, Laura was not burning.

"Begone," I murmured, surprising myself. "Begone," I said again, a bit louder. What was I doing? Without any answer, I stepped into the room, into the phantom fire, directly into the middle of it, turned in place, surveying the phenomenon. Again, no heat, no fire. All imaginary. Or was it? It wasn't anything I was prepared for—who could be prepared for such a thing? Roman, of course; but I wasn't Roman. I was poor, mortal Valerie and I began to shrink from the task before me.

I had to quell the thing, whatever it was. Nothing else was as important as that. I had to stop it.

"Begone!" I yelled, and a tiny voice inside my mind asked me who I thought I was. Nothing happened. The fire remained, except I began to feel a new sensation: heat. Actual heat, and real smoke. It stung my eyes, made me cough. I tried to focus on the girl and leapt over to her bed and to her side. She didn't respond to my touch or the calling of her name, so I shook her and then, hating the idea of it, slapped her face, once, twice. Still there was no response. Laura Clowers was dead to the world.

Panic gripped me. What was I to do? The bedclothes began to smolder and wisps of smoke rose up from them. The phantom fire still raged, numbing my vision with its chaos, but every other of my senses screamed that the blaze would soon be all too real, and we both would be all too consumed.

Oh, Dear One; I admit it to you: I gave in. I leaned over the girl to cover her the best I could with my own body and hugged her to me, any strength I once had to attempt to pull her out of the room gone from me, a victim of the strange phenomenon all around me.

I waited for the end, my eyes squeezed shut and every nerve in my body telling me that to die by fire would be one of the most terrible ways of all to die.

Far off, my name was being called. Hands grabbed my shoulders, then my waist in an effort to move me off the bed. Inwardly, I prayed it was Roman, but something told me it couldn't possibly be him. He was busy elsewhere. He was *needed* elsewhere.

"Valerie, look."

And I looked. I opened my eyes and found them filled with my own tears, but whole and with sight. The first thing I saw was Laura's pale, unmoving face right in front of me, but I moved, slowly, and someone helped me to sit up, turning me to survey the room.

The room was not burning, nor was it burnt.

Roman lifted me to my feet, asking if I was okay. I nodded to him and then collapsed into his arms, my face buried in his shoulder. I wept and wept and wept until finally the emotion left me completely and I pulled myself together to check on the girl. Laura Clowers, I found, was still dead to the world, but not literally dead, Roman told me.

"We should leave this room now," he said, and determining the fact that I could stand and presumably walk on my own without help, he crouched down to take the girl up into his arms and directed me to please open the door. I walked over to it, grasped the handle, turned it, and opened the door. I was facing Roman when I did so, and he was facing the now-open portal.

"*Close the door!*" he bellowed.

Diary, please do not hold me to the few minutes or more that followed. My recall of them is corrupted and I cannot trust that everything I'm to tell you is accurate. I remember hearing Roman tell me to shut the door, but my arms were like stone, and my head like a lead weight. I do recall him stepping forward, though, with Laura still in his arms, and kicking the door out of my hand and closed. The sound of it should have rung through the little stateroom, but for some reason it closed with a dull thud. I looked at it just as dully, then to Roman—I couldn't comprehend what was happening, not then, not even now.

The next thing I knew—if I even know what I'm writing about—was a horrible rapping on the outer side of the door, as if someone was beating at it repeatedly with a piece of metal. I thought I saw the wood of the door actually push inward toward us, but again I cannot be sure such a vision occurred. What I do remember clearly is the horrible sounds of someone trying to get through that door.

Roman stepped back and set the girl back on the bed. He grabbed my arm and drew me across the floor and to her—or did I do that on my own? Still, I landed on top of her, or at least partly so, and was told not to look. In my own right mind such a command would have been challenged, but with my body barely responding to me and my head hung so low as to bend my neck permanently, I obeyed Roman and buried my face next to Laura's, frightened and bewildered.

In an instant, my ears were assailed by the most terrifying of sounds. The door creaking as if to break any second. Roman shouting for someone to stay back. Heavy footfalls. A low, inhuman moan that increased to a keening wail. Roman again ordering someone to not advance further, to "leave this plane," and to return to wherever it or he or whatever was appropriate came from. And then, most horrible of all, the sound of gunfire, loud and near deafening in the tiny space.

I prayed to survive the encounter. I prayed for the fire not to return. I prayed for my soul, for Roman's, and for Laura Clowers'. In the middle of the maelstrom, I couldn't see how any of us would survive.

Then, from somewhere deep inside me, my normal personality asserted itself and I opened one eye to spy on the situation.

Roman was close to us, so very close, leaning backward at an angle that defied the laws of the physical world, and wrestling with something—someone. Whatever or whoever it was, I couldn't see. I might have been dreaming it all, hallucinating, but I was sure that the girl was beneath me and I was holding her close to me. That much I knew and know for certain now as I write this.

There was a sudden movement in the middle of the struggle—Roman's arm shot out, disentangling itself from the hold it was stuck in, and in the hand at the end of the arm the fingers gripped a small, thick disc. Roman's disc...talisman...weapon...what have you. I don't know what to call it. I had only ever seen it once before, and he had only ever actually spoken about it to me on one occasion.

"The Eye of God." His words returned to me, the words he used to describe the disc after he'd, well, returned from...death. "The Face of the Divine, that singular sight which no spirits can bear."

My own spirit rallied! If it was a nightmare I was caught in, I could see an end to it! If the monstrous ghost that assaulted us was to look upon the disc, it would not stand! I trusted in that, clung to it, while the world crumbled all around me there in that room aboard this train at that horrible moment.

A great smacking sound exploded in my ears, and the disc went sailing through the air to impact a wall of Laura's room and fall somewhere out of sight. I looked up at Roman with both eyes and met his for a single, precious moment. Darkness followed and an end to all sensation.

I—have to stop here, Dear One. My hands are trembling too violently.

Valerie

Assistant Conductor - Day Log
June 10

Just minutes before my shift was ending, I was informed by the conductor of an incident in Car 7 involving Mr. Clowers, his daughter, and Sgt. Janus. I am unsure of the details due to the conductor being unsure of them, also, but I understand there to have been an altercation between the two men that somehow also involved Mrs. Havelock-Mayer. The result, I'm told, is that the daughter has been injured in some fashion and there is also evidence of fire in the girl's room.

While I am of course concerned for the passengers' well-being at all times, reports of a fire are also concerning due to the incident just yesterday with the stove. In all, the conductor is of the opinion to revoke the tickets of all the parties and put them off the train at our next stop. I am leaving now to see if I can learn more about the situation, and have been forewarned that Mr. Clowers is threatening legal action against Sgt. Janus and Mrs. Havelock-Mayer and to be cautious of doing or saying anything to make matters worse.

If I may note it here, I spoke at length with Janus earlier today and found him to be a forthright gentleman and not the type to use violence. I could not say the same for Mr. Clowers.

CROSS-COUNTRY LTD - 10 JUNE

TO: MRS. DANIEL CLOWERS
WEYFORTH, THE CITY

EMILY

LAURA HURT AND UNCONSCIOUS. DO NOT KNOW
WHY EXACTLY BUT STRANGE MAN ON TRAIN AP-
PEARS RESPONSIBLE. AM LOOKING INTO IT AND DO
NOT WORRY. WILL SPEED LAURA HOME WITH ALL
HASTE. AM ALSO CONTACTING SHOTTEN AS SOON
AS POSSIBLE FOR LEGAL ACTION AND REPARA-
TIONS. AGAIN DO NOT WORRY. I AM HANDLING THE
MATTER. KEEP EVERYTHING TO YOURSELF ONLY,
MUST NOT GO PUBLIC WITH ANY OF IT. MOST IM-
PORTANT.

DANIEL

June 10th

Arthur,

I probably shouldn't say this on the back of a postcard, but there has been a big to-do on the train between these people Linda and I met at dinner yesterday evening. I'm not sure what it's all about but a young girl's in the middle of it somehow and I think she's sick or hurt—probably a *drug addict*. I can't believe it would happen on *our* train, but it is sort-of exciting. Hope to tell you more when I'm home, if I ever *get* home again.

Love,

Lydia

Dear Diary,

Let me try to bring you up to date before we go to—well, let me start at the beginning. Or where I left off before, I mean. I'm not sure exactly what I mean, because it's been a long night.

I must have fainted or passed out again, and when I awoke, Roman had removed me to my room. Before he could say anything, or most likely stand pat on *not* saying anything, I demanded answers from him on what had happened at Laura's room. What I am about to write is as near to verbatim as I can recall of our conversation.

"Do you know the story of Virginia Jordan?" he began. When after a moment of thought I admitted the name seemed very familiar, he nodded and said, "It was roughly thirty years ago when the girl, an heiress to the—"

"Jordan Iron Works fortune," I interrupted, finally catching up with him. "Yes, I do remember. The girl who was abducted from her family home and who surprised everyone by not trying to escape her captor, but joined him in his career."

"As a notorious bandit," Roman added, a grim look on his face. I could see the stress and strain of the last…hour? Few hours? I was unaware of how much time had passed since the attack by the—the *thing*.

He went on. "Clement Lee Chase, known as simply 'Chase' to those who followed his 'adventures,' and those who championed him as a 19th century Robin Hood. He was, in fact, considered to be one of the very worst criminals of his day, and an unrepentant killer."

It was all coming back to me. I was just a schoolgirl at the time, but my parents talked more than once about the incident of the Jordan girl's kidnapping, and my classmates and I discussed it on the playground. I admit that it had a nebulous romantic thread running through it that appealed to young females—myself included—but we didn't know then of the full heinous nature of the bandit's beatings and killings. I suppose as children we were being shielded from the worst aspects of his career.

I thought for a moment about Virginia Jordan. She was only a few years older than me when she was taken, nearly a teenager.

What made her not only agree to stay with Chase, but, as some reports declared, become a willing accomplice?

"Oh, no, Roman," I said, looking up at him with a sudden thought. "You mean to say that spirit is…"

"Yes, Valerie. I'm almost certain of it. It's Clement Chase—or the part of him that still clings to this plane."

It was terrifying, the idea that such a man, a murderer of cold fashion, one of the most accomplished criminals of the last, oh, hundred years, could step forward from death and continue his rampage in the waking world.

"But *why*, Roman?"

I saw that my question surprised him. He often forgets that the rest of us are not always aware of the answers he is already aware of.

"Think of the story," he urged me. "The girl spent years with him, by his side for robberies, assaults, and murders. The police could not catch them, nor even government agents, and they seemed to be untouchable—until the day Virginia Jordan left Chase."

"And she went home," I added, remembering more of it. "Her father took her back, and she was never charged with any crime. Oh, talk then was that Jordan paid heavily to insure she never saw the harsher side of a cell door, but however it transpired the girl went scot free."

Roman shook his head and ran his fingers through his hair. "No, not scot free entirely, if you recall. This fact is most important to our current situation: Jordan began to move her around all across the country. Why? To stay one step ahead of Chase. Why again? Because Chase would not let her go."

The horror of it crashed over me, threatening to upset what little foundation I was standing on—am still standing on. "He's *here*, now, looking for her?"

Roman nodded silently, then opened both hands to bare his palms, as if to bid me to continue my thoughts.

"Good Lord, Roman; he thinks she's *here*. On this train. All because of…Laura Clowers."

"No, not entirely, my dear. Chase is already linked to this train.

Laura only opened up a path for him to access it…something he's been waiting for a long time." I shook my head, not comprehending exactly what he meant, so he continued. "Earlier, I learned things from our friend Mr. Butters, the conductor, as I questioned him in a way to dredge up information I could use to see into the heart of this matter. Do you know how Clement Chase died?"

I assured him I didn't; in fact, I believed no one did beyond rumors. I remembered stories of him ultimately being caught, of being hanged, even of his taking his own life as the law closed in on him.

"He died right here on this train, Valerie. In a fire."

I couldn't talk. I couldn't form words. My tongue was made of stone. Roman saw this and reached out to take my hand as he went on.

"Chase somehow discovered the fact that Virginia Jordan was on this train and swooped in to take her away again. But, a fire broke out—no one knows how—and the bandit died in it."

"And the girl?" I asked, finding words again.

Roman frowned. "I don't know. Butters didn't know, either. But he did tell me all about how the cars that burnt up in the fire were reused. The actual steel platforms, the wheels, the shell of it, all reused to make new cars. *These* cars. Very few people know that. It's not something the railroad company is keen to be made public."

We sat without speaking for a few minutes, I with my thoughts, trying to piece it all together, and Roman presumably with his much clearer thoughts, most likely waiting for me to catch up with him.

Catch up with him. Like Virginia Jordan waiting for Chase the murdering bandit to catch up to her.

"Who did Laura actually contact, then? With her board?"

Roman gave me a slight smile. "A very astute question, Valerie. One might assume Chase, but I now have equal reason to believe it might have been the Jordan girl. If so, the bandit was, if you'll forgive me, a 'bonus.'"

"If," I began, hesitantly, "Laura contacted Virginia…does that mean she died here on this train?"

"Yes," said Roman. "Very likely yes."

I took a breath and held it. There were more things I wanted to ask him, things that I felt would help me understand what was happening, or, yes, might even make things more confusing. I had to *know*, though, because I was in the middle of it. I was involved.

I found the story of Chase and Virginia still fascinated me as much now as did when I was a girl, but I made up my mind to ask Roman how we'd gotten away from the gunfighting ghost not once, but now twice. It seemed remarkable to me, especially since my companion had been, well, down in the dumps, chagrined actually, about *something* since our first encounter.

As Fate would have it, a knock at the door just as I opened my mouth to ask interrupted our little chat. Roman got up to answer it and found Daniel Clowers standing there in the corridor with strange eyes and none of the bluster about him as before.

Once invited in, he began to talk. He informed us that Laura was comatose, but had no signs of violence upon her or apparent illness or, I suppose most importantly to the man, no needle marks. She was simply unmoving, unresponsive, without signs of life save for her breathing.

Clowers himself looked quite awful. He's been taken down a peg; that I could clearly see. He'd been *shown something* that gave him pause. He saw his daughter at what appeared to be the edge of death. Roman did not crow; that's not his way. He simply listened to the man talk, nodding now and then, and raising an eyebrow at certain points. I could see sympathy in him, but forgive me, I didn't feel much of it myself.

"You said something the other night, at dinner," Clowers told Roman when asked what he could do for the politician. Instead of getting to it, he then insisted on a brief diatribe that basically accused Roman of inspiring Laura's use of the Ouija board—the political attack dog was never too far from the surface, apparently. Roman took it in stride, knowing full well as I did that the girl was already deep into Spiritualist practices before we ever met her here on this train. He must have spotted my hackles rising to debate Clowers, and laid a hand on my arm to let me know to contain myself while he brushed off the damning words and asked again what he could do for father and daughter.

48

Clowers leaned forward. "You said 'Though we cannot know the mind of God, we can feel assured that his hand is always in ours.' Furthermore, you intimated you yourself are one of His instruments here on Earth—I sense that in you, sir. Once I observed my daughter and realized that there is something entirely...*wrong* about her state, I began to reorganize my thoughts about you. I feel now as I can afford to ask you to look in on her." He closed his eyes tightly for a moment, then reopened them to look directly into Roman's, as if searching his soul. "Will you?"

Without pause, without hesitation, Roman replied "of course."

Clowers stood up, glancing at me for the briefest of moments, and walked to the door. Turning, he skewered us both with a cold look.

"But God help you if you hurt her further."

And so, Dear One, we are now leaving our rooms to see the girl. Roman told me he needed some time to prepare himself, but he is ready now. I hope that I am also ready.

Valerie

Assistant Conductor – Day Log
June 11

It is early morning before I go on duty, but Sgt. Janus has asked me to be present while he looks in on Mr. Clowers' daughter, who I believe is very ill. I am told I can serve as a "neutral party" by the sergeant, though I don't exactly know what he means by that.

Still, I see no harm in it and I will be off-duty. If it means an easing of the tensions between him and Mr. Clowers, I believe I could be of some help in being present.

Because it involves something private between passengers and does not harm the train or the company, I am not notifying the conductor of the event at this time.

CROSS-COUNTRY LTD - 11 JUNE

TO: MRS. DANIEL CLOWERS
WEYFORTH, THE CITY

EMILY

IGNORE LAST TELEGRAM. LAURA STILL NOT RE-
SPONSIVE BUT HAVE THE SITUATION TIGHTLY UN-
DER CONTROL. HAVE HAD A CHANGE OF HEART
THAT DON'T FULLY COMPREHEND BUT AM TRYING
SOMETHING ELSE. IF IT DOESN'T WORK, WILL STILL
SPEED HOME WITH HER. TRUST ME. DO NOTHING
AT THIS TIME. TALK TO NO ONE ABOUT THIS. WILL
CONTACT YOU SOON WITH MORE INFORMATION.

DANIEL

Dear Diary,

I will try to give you some of the details of our examination of the girl, Laura Clowers, now, but bear with me because I am bone-tired.

Surprisingly, her father had moved her to his own room and that is where we saw her. A cloud hung over us as we entered the room, mostly due to Daniel Clowers' strange mood and willingness to allow Roman to examine Laura. I wish I knew what had compelled him, but at that moment we tried to concentrate on the girl's unfortunate state.

I was also surprised to see the Negro conductor, Butters, join us, and equally surprised to hear that it was Roman who invited him. It was explained to me that the man would serve as a kind of chaperone, a witness of sorts on neither "side" of the argument. What exactly Roman saw in the conductor I couldn't say, but I suspect he'd favorably made up his mind about him when they'd met earlier while I slept.

Noting a light tic and even slighter raised eyebrow from Clowers upon Butters' entrance, I sat down near Laura's still figure on the bed and watched as Roman also sat down on the opposite side and took the girl's hand in his. Her father hovered over us; I could feel his eyes follow every single movement we made.

Roman shook his head and set Laura's hand back down at her side. Then he leaned over and turned her head toward him. None of this elicited any response whatsoever from her. She continued to sleep, her eyes closed and her breathing very shallow. Roman frowned and with his fingers very delicately opened both her eyelids. Clowers sucked in his breath at this, but I refused to look up at him—he'd asked Roman there and would have to let things happen as they will.

"She's not there," Roman said quietly as he sat up straight again after staring deeply into the girl's eyes for nearly a full minute.

The politician immediately demanded to know what that meant, but my companion ignored him for the most part, merely raising one hand briefly to silence the man. Then, he leaned down to look again, this time for almost five full minutes. One might think having to watch such an act would be tedious, but the three of us—myself, Clowers, and the conductor—watched intently and silently. For my own part, I hung on every second, expecting Roman to shout suddenly at some discovery or another. But, he didn't. After five minutes he ceased looking at whatever he was looking at in the girl's eyes and sat up again. This time he turned to the father to speak.

"I was wrong, Mr. Clowers. Please accept my apology if I caused you any distress. Laura *is* there, but only in a very small way..."

At this point I noticed Clowers' hands trembling. He tried to raise one to wipe at his brow, but he couldn't get it to perform as it should, apparently. Instead he again demanded to know what Roman meant by that. I admit the answer Roman gave him was frustrating, and *I* know how he is normally.

He said without emotion, "Laura is there, but she's not alone. In fact, the two of them seem to be *hiding*."

Clowers sputtered and grimaced, and I did actually feel some small sympathy for him in the light of Roman's reply. To try and mediate the situation, I held up a hand to the politician and got Roman's attention to ask him to attempt to explain to us what he meant, but in a way Laura's father might more easily understand. As soon as the words left my mouth I bit my lip, hoping I hadn't spoken as a parent to a wayward child and hurt Roman's feelings. Thankfully, he didn't bat an eye at it.

"Laura's...soul," he said, looking back and forth between Clowers and me, "for lack of a better term, is nearly gone from her body. It only exists on the outermost fringes of it. This can occur after a highly traumatic event, either physical or para-physical, which is understandable, really. She's barely there, in herself. Just barely."

"And she's not alone?" I asked.

He shook his head, looking back at the girl with curiosity. "No, there's another soul there with her, but also just barely." Roman looked at me abruptly. "Valerie, I think it's Virginia Jordan."

Before I could say anything, Daniel Clowers roared "Who the *hell* is Virginia Jordan?"

With a silent nod from Roman, I related the story of the Jordan heiress and her bandit to the politician, or at least all I knew then of the events. As I spoke, I happened to glance over at Butters and saw him nodding to me, as if confirming each part of the tale as it was told. I knew then what he and Roman had talked about previously in their meeting.

When I was done, Clowers turned away for a moment to stand with his back to us, not saying anything or moving. After a long moment he looked back to us, thanked us for coming, and said he needed time to think. Would we please leave and wait for him to contact us again?

We all rose and exited the room, leaving the man to his thoughts, whatever they were at that time.

Valerie

Dear Granny Mima,

I wanted to tell you of happenings on my train.

I met a hoodoo man, and he is much like what you told me about such persons. I believe him to be a good man, kind and smart, but he carries great burdens on him and bad things follow him around. In fact, there are bad things going on right now as I write this. A girl has been stricken with a powerful malady and will not wake. The hoodoo man has looked into her, exactly as the way you once described to me when I was a boy, and he has found so much that is wrong.

Beyond that, I believe the Devil himself has come to the train.

I will go about my duties best I can, because that is what you taught me. I want to do right by you and all you did for me. You pushed me to learning and schooling, though you didn't have any yourself, not the proper kind at least. You were so happy and proud when I took the job on my train. That was a good day. I hope this train can move past the dark that has come aboard her and we can have good days again.

Granny Mima, I miss you something mighty, and think of you nearly every day. I know you will never see this letter, but writing it has given me a powerful feeling of peace and I hope I can write you again. I may need your help and advice in the days to come if I'm to be able to help the hoodoo man.

Now, I have to go to my job and my duties.

Love,

Gabriel

June 11th

Arthur,

Well, I'm sure seeing this letter has knocked you onto your keister, dear, but what I have to tell you is too much for a post-card! And to wait until I'm home—you remember I'm going off to Mother's and not straight back to you? Well, anyway, here it all is just as it happened:

Linda and I were just sitting there finishing up our late break-fast when the man I met the other night—the one I told you was involved in some trouble?—came right up to us and asked me if I'd like to be part of a séance? Can you believe that? Just bold-facedly asked me! And before you even think of it, Linda was not asked, and the way she's acting toward me I'd be surprised if she ever spoke to me again. As if I did something to be asked and she wasn't!

Well, sir, this Sgt. Janus—that's the man's name, kind of an odd duck who wears a military uniform, but it has no marks on it—what do they call them? Signs? Stripes? Anyway, he's handsome in a rough way, with the most strange eyes. Not just the color, but how he looks right through you. That's the only way I can describe it! He said something about how the "circle needs another female" and it would help "strengthen the sympathetic call" he wanted to put out. Isn't that just the most? Well, I said yes, of course!

Now, I know you're sitting there and raising your eyebrows, dear, because you know I never did truck with all that Spiritualist non-sense and ooga-booga, and I don't believe Mr. Houdini really does have any magical powers or whatnot, but it is a new experience and you know I'm always up for those! How could I say no? Now, af-terward, I'm glad I went along like a good sport, though there were some very, very strange moments in that room, I can tell you.

What happened then was this…

Sgt. Janus told me what room to go to and at what time. When I arrived he greeted me at the door, which turned out to be the room of a young girl Linda and I met the other night, the daughter of that

Clowers man, you know the one, the politician? I can't remember his first name, but it doesn't really matter because his girl is the one I told you I think is a *drug addict*. If that's the case, Mr. Clowers has a world of troubles on his doorstep I don't care to even think about.

So, it was the sergeant and the politician and his daughter Laura—who was sleeping when I came in. She was unconscious, that much I know! There was also another lady there, another person I met the other night who had a long last name I didn't quite catch, but her first name was Valerie. Pretty, with long red hair—I'd guess she's about forty? Cold manners and a bit uppity, if you know what I mean, but didn't say much the whole time, just kept staring at Sgt. Janus, which I take to mean she's sweet on him. He doesn't strike me as being too overly sweet on her, or at least not like the way she'd like.

There was also a *colored man*, one of the conductors. I wish I knew why he was there, but maybe to keep an eye on things for the railroad? I don't believe I was told his name, though he seemed to know mine. I guess it's his job, of course, but really…

Arthur, I know what you're saying now: What did Lydia get herself into? But don't mind anything of what I tell you like that. It wasn't anything *illegal* or improper or anything at all for you to worry yourself over. Your wife knows what kinds of things to not get mixed up in, and this was something I just didn't want to miss, in spite of all the strangers around me…emphasis on *strange*!

So, first Sgt. Janus tells this Clowers to trust him, that he knows what he's doing. That man sort-of grumbled and glowered but let him go ahead. Then, they set the girl up in a chair around a table! Yes, she was still sleeping! This Valerie and I were asked to sit on either side of the girl and take her hands in ours! I hoped her hand wasn't going to be cold and clammy, but it was warm, very nice and warm, so I did it after sitting down in my own chair. The politician sat next to me—had to take my other hand!—and the colored conductor was between him and Sgt. Janus, who was next to Valerie. A neat little circle of friends!

The séance began after we were all sitting and the lights dimmed. It was just as I always had heard, quiet and spooky, with all of us being told to "concentrate," though I wasn't sure on what. Fortunately, the sergeant has such a nice voice, manly but peaceful when he wants to, the kind of a voice that could put you to sleep if you listened in a certain way. Why, I had to work to not fall asleep myself! And do you know what? When it began and he started talking I almost forgot we were on a train!

He started off saying we probably all knew by now what happens in these things, how we're supposed to act because it's been in so many newspapers and books and plays by now. Everybody nodded and looked like they understood, and I took it to mean we were to be quiet and watch for signs and such. Then the sergeant asked if "you are there, Virginia"! I don't know who exactly she was, but Sgt. Janus was very certain she was somewhere out there—and he got his answer when the girl Laura answered "yes"! Could have knocked me over with a feather! I thought she was asleep!

His friend Valerie seemed pretty excited about it, but he hushed her and moved on to ask if Laura was there, which was queer to me because I was holding her hand! Of course she was there! And yes, the girl spoke after a very long moment that she was there, but her voice sounded like it was quite a way's off, very small and quiet, not like the girl just wasn't putting anything behind it, but like she really was...well, very far away. Very, very far away. And I have to tell you: Her voice was *different from the other one*! The one that answered for Virginia!

Sgt. Janus told her she needed to come back, and he said it gently, but also in a way that came across like he meant business. And that she needed to bring Virginia with her! Oh, I'm getting all upset and in a dither just thinking about it to tell you...especially now I'm up to the first very, very, very strange thing that happened—one of the girls then said, "*He's coming...*"

Do you know what Sgt. Janus did then when he heard that? And this Valerie, too? They both jumped a little. Now, not very much because they still held each other's hands and those next to them, but it was almost like I felt some alarm, some jolt of caution *through the circle*! And then suddenly the sergeant says, "Listen! Can you hear that?"

but I didn't hear anything, not a blessed thing. Valerie says *she* can and so did that colored conductor, but myself and Mr. Clowers both told them *we* couldn't hear anything and what did they hear? The sergeant says he could hear footsteps, like boots on a wooden floor, and then all of a sudden he says it's *a door opening somewhere!*

Why, sir, I looked around expecting to see the door to the room open, but it did not. The two of them, Sgt. Janus and his friend, are getting more excited each second and then he warns us to not let go of the other person's hand and "*the circle must be unbroken!*"

Maybe it reflects poor on me, Arthur, but I admit that right then and there I almost started singing that hymn from about twenty years ago—you know the one? But I didn't because everybody else was taking the whole thing very seriously, which brings me right up to what happened with the politician Clowers.

Up to that point he'd been fairly quiet, not saying much of anything and calm and composed in the face of what was happening with his daughter. I thought it mighty strange considering he seemed hostile to me when we first gathered—oh, I mean hostile to the room, not to me specifically. Like he was against the whole séance, but was going ahead with it anyway to please Sgt. Janus. It wasn't any of my bee's wax, so I just set it aside, but when we were told someone was coming, the man up and says in a very straight, even voice, "*I'm already here*"!

Well! I nearly jumped out of my skin, husband! All of a sudden the sergeant shouts, "Let go of him, Mrs. Basch!" and of course I did, *but he didn't let go of me!* I didn't know what to do! But before I could barely think, Sgt. Janus leaned over to us from across the table and made a chopping motion with his hand and hit Clowers right on his—the one holding mine. It was like lightning! And then that man let go of me and it was like I wasn't even there anymore, and the only one in the room to him was the sergeant.

"She's gone, Chase," said Sgt. Janus, his voice all serious and his eyes like fire. "There's nothing here for you." But the politician just looks around the room and right through the rest of us until his eyes meet back up with the sergeant's, who, I swear it's true, said

"Begone!" just like in some of those Bible plays. Do you know what Clowers does then? He starts shaking all over, like he was cold with chills and Sgt. Janus then said, "Fight it, Daniel! Fight him!" To tell you I was confused and not sure if I was coming or going at that point would be an understatement!

So then Mr. Clowers breaks out in a terrible sweat and his arms are moving and he's still shaking, but his feet are rooted to the floor like his boots were nailed down. I see the sergeant reach into his pocket then, as if he's going to take something from it, but he didn't and stepped over to the politician to take him by the shoulders and said it again: "Begone!"

And he went. Whoever "he" was. Someone named Chase, apparently.

The room got deathly quiet then, and we all, well, picked up the pieces, I guess. The girl Laura was fast asleep again and Valerie took her to the bed. Clowers just sat there and stared at the table while Sgt. Janus ministered to him. The conductor took a few steps back and looked ill at ease and nervous about something. I figured it was all over and I was ready to call it a day when Valerie opened the shade on the window and we saw it was already *dusk*! As if hours and hours had passed instead of minutes! I could figure for it, Arthur, and still can't. But it wasn't over. Just as I got up to thank my hosts for a very strange time, the other shoe dropped.

Laura, the girl who was dead to the world, picks her head up off the pillow and said in a very clear, but very odd voice, "Don't tell him—I'm going home."

With that I had had enough. Do you blame me? And so here I am back in my room with Linda still pouting and me writing the longest letter I've ever written. And the kicker is that now I feel like maybe it was all just a big parlor game, just like all those Spiritualists Mr. Houdini is exposing. Oh, well, at least they didn't ask me for any money.

Love,

Lydia

P.S. I promise to only write postcards from here on out.

Dear Diary,

The séance is over, and we're worse for wear for it, not better.
Oh, I just realized I didn't say anything about a séance before.
My mind is all mixed up, still confused. Much time has passed without us knowing and matters are far from good. In fact, I'd say we're in quite a pickle.

We held a séance in Clowers' room to try and get to the bottom of it all, to find out what's happened to Laura primarily, and to some extent Virginia Jordan, also. It didn't go the way Roman had hoped, or what I believe he'd hoped. It only provided us with the fact that Laura Clowers may be lost to her father and irretrievable. I pray that's not the case, though, but Chase showed himself during the séance and spooked the life out of me…and I'm one who's faced down my own dearly departed father, a tyrant of not small proportions.

Here's what's happened:

The girl is now barely breathing, just enough to sustain life, but shallow and at times ragged. Her countenance is pale and dusky around the edges. She won't respond to anything and Roman fears that the longer her soul is nearly absent from her body the closer she travels toward death.

Travel. That's the word for it. It seems Virginia, for whatever reasons, has taken Laura as a kind of traveling companion—that's how Roman explained it to me—and gone home. But we don't rightfully know where "home" is, and the girl is slipping farther and farther away with each passing minute. Her father is not much better; since being possessed by Chase—yes, I know how that sounds—he himself is barely cohesive and walking around more like the living dead than a normal man.

How much worse could it be? Well, Dear One, there's more.

After we returned to his room following the séance, Roman's sense of urgency peaked to the point that I saw an opening to ask again about what it is that's been bothering him apart from, of course, the larger events of our journey on this wretched, cursed train. Thankfully, he told me…or perhaps I'm not thankful for it. It

61

seems to be a matter of despair for him. You see, "The Eye of God" is not working as it usually does...

Wait—someone's at the door. It's the conductor, Butters. Roman is letting him in...the man looks awful. Something else has occurred. I will tell you when I can.

Valerie

Dear Granny Mima,

I have sinned, and for my sins I have been punished.

I tried to help the hoodoo man. He asked me to sit with him and his company for a contact and I did, but time passed strangely and when the contact was done I had lost hours, and they were hours I owed to the railroad.

Just now, I was told that my services are no longer required. I asked how that could be, as I have always given my all to my duty on the train, but the answer was not clear. Only that I had been shirking that duty and being lazy and late—and now I have no job, no position, after years of work.

Oh, Mima, I am ashamed to tell you this. I thought to help someone in need, but now there is no help for me. I don't know what I am going to do, because the railroad has been my life. What good is what I know and what I can do if I cannot put it to use?

Still, I think of you and your hardships and how you never lay down and never gave in. You taught me these things, and I have carried them with me all the time I have been apart from you.

Times are strange aboard this train. It is under a bad sign, perhaps many bad signs. I have heard the Devil speak today and I am moved to stop him somehow, but now without my position I don't see how I can. It is a bad day.

All I can see being able to do now is to go to the hoodoo man and his lady and tell them I can no longer help them, for I must try and help myself until once again in a way that I can help others.

And I will forever be wary of just how far I go to help. I feel that what I have already done may have helped the Devil to walk this train.

Love,

Gabriel

Dear Diary,

Events are piling up one on top of another now and I'm not sure how much more our little band can endure. I say "band" because we are now more than just Roman and myself. Let me try to explain.

It is late in the day—is it the third or fourth since we left the conference? I'm afraid I'm not even sure anymore, so much has transpired and so much of it dark and murky in my mind. We have taken rooms in a small inn across from the train station in—I have to try to remember the town's name—Horton Corners, that's it—and the rooms give us a good view of the train. Our train. The train that will not run.

They say it just stopped, and that we were fortunate to have enough forward momentum to reach this town and its station. Even now I can look out the windows of our third-floor rooms and see men pouring over the locomotive and walking up and down its length as it sits there like a lead paperweight on the tracks, silent and unmoving. Once urging all passengers to either sit tight while repairs are being made or find alternate transportation to finish their journeys, the conductor told Roman that there is nothing apparently wrong with it. It simply will not run.

Roman, I'm sure, knows why, but he's holding his own counsel on that because he has much more pressing matters to wrestle with. Let me think over them and attempt to sort through them for you.

The Clowers are with us, father and daughter. Laura is still comatose and breathing shallowly, and her father is walking and talking, but only when prompted. Otherwise he mostly sits there dully, his eyes staring off into the distance and his entire expression one of—well, he has no real expression, I guess. I don't have a clue what's going on in his head.

We are stymied with Laura. Roman says her soul, most of it, is gone, spirited away by Virginia Jordan, a girl who died decades ago. And to where? "Home" is all we know, and that for now is a mystery. I've wracked my brains to dredge up that part of the story, where she came from, but to no avail. Horton Corners is too small, too insular to have the resources we need to find out, and Roman says we cannot go elsewhere; Laura cannot be moved and something must be done very soon to save her life.

The other member of our band is Gabriel Butters, former head conductor of the train that has abandoned us, and we it. The Negro came to us informing Roman he'd been sacked by the railroad for his failure to appear for his duties, despite the fact that he like the rest of us lost time somehow due to the séance. I assume his employers were less than encouraged by said excuse, if the man even bothered to use it. When Butters told Roman he could no longer help him, my companion simply looked him in the eye and proclaimed, "Nonsense. You now work for me."

And here we are, sequestered in an inn in a strange town with a girl's life hanging in the balance and as evil a restless spirit as Sgt. Janus claims to ever have encountered in his career.

"Chase is without a conscience, without scruples, and without any sort of belief system save whatever he may have created for himself long ago," Roman told me as we looked out the window a few minutes ago at the train. "He's godless, Valerie. He has separated himself from the Deity to the extent of not being subject to this." He held up that disc of his in his palm, its face hidden as it always is, except for when Roman needs to present it to break a spirit's ties to the mortal plane.

Listen to me; I'm writing such things as if completely natural to me. What am I becoming?

After sitting and writing on a pad of paper taken from his jacket, the ex-conductor is now up and pacing the floor, which seems odd for him, though there's little I actually know about him. Roman is about to speak to him; I believe he thinks the man has something to tell us. Whatever it may be, I pray it isn't more bad news.

Valerie

Dear Granny Mima,

Your life was now so long ago, but I remember you telling me of the Time of No Choice and what it was to be born into it. Those memories you passed to me and I will never forget them. Now, I have a Time of Choice, and this at least makes my heart glad.

You see, the hoodoo man, who I will no longer call that: he is Sgt. Roman Janus, a good man, has taken me into his kindness and offered me a job with him. I don't know what kind of a job yet, but he's truthful in his words and I believe he can put me to use. He doesn't care what color a man's skin is, or where his family is from. His woman, though, I am not sure feels the same, but she is not evil so I feel I can allow myself to trust her, too.

Granny Mima, I also remember you saying that when one dances on the edge of a knife, one can either feel the knife then at their back or in their hand. Because I now have Choice, I choose to feel it in my hand, though you know in my heart I am not a violent man. Still, the time has come to be of use again, and with the way things are around me now, I want to be able to have the knife where I can see it and use it if necessary.

Knowledge can be a knife, and I have knowledge that may be of use to Sgt. Janus. I am ready to tell him things I know, because I have listened to him talk of his problems, and they are many and heavy, and some of them I may be able to unburden him with.

Be with me, Granny, as you were when I was a boy. The speeding train is coming, and maybe some of it is of my own doing, but I want to meet it as a man.

The Lord God help me if it leads to *wimbo wa treni ya giza*, for that is something I do not care to meet.

Love,

Gabriel

LILAC INN, HORTON CORNERS, COUNTY PETER –
JUNE 13

TO: MR JOSHUA HARGREAVES
MOUNT AIRY, TROUGHTON HOUSE

JOSHUA,

MOST URGENT, GIRLS LIFE IN MORTAL DANGER.
GO TO MY LIBRARY, SECOND CASE ON WEST WALL,
THIRD SHELF. TAKE BOOK 'PORTUS TEMPESTATE,
VOL 2' AND SEND TO ME AT ABOVE ADDRESS.
ALL HASTE. SPARE NO EXPENSE. CANNOT STRESS
ENOUGH. PLACE ALL TRUST IN YOU ON THIS.

JANUS

Dear Diary,

Roman has just come in and he has his teeth in something. I can see it in his face, and it gives me some hope.

The events of the past few hours have been monumental in the grand scheme of things, and I'll try to reconstruct them here for you.

First, as I said before, Roman approached Butters to urge the man to talk if he had something to say. Feeling like a fly on the wall that might hear things I shouldn't, I took the opportunity to get up and look in on Laura. She was in exactly the same state as she'd been for hours—days?—but looking at her, simply gazing at her young, pretty features, something clicked in me. I cannot explain it but I remembered where Virginia Jordan was from.

Flying back to Roman, I told him breathlessly that the girl was from Jordan, which was her father's town… a "company town," in fact, named for their family and for their business, built specifically for the company's employees with everything they'd need in their daily lives beyond their jobs. Jordan, the town Virginia was abducted from, and for whatever reason, ran back to after leaving Chase.

And now, supposedly, where she was heading once more—but with Laura in tow.

Roman looked from me to Butters upon hearing the news. "You knew of this?" The ex-conductor shook his head and turned away from us. Roman looked back to me, his eyes full of thanks. "That's it, then," he said. "That's where she's going, and where I need to go to catch up to her."

I asked him why he thought she'd left the bandit after having joined him in his life of crime.

"I don't, Valerie," he said, shrugging his shoulders. "But the answer is in Jordan; I'm sure of it. I just have to get there."

"You can't," Butters told him, suddenly speaking up. Roman asked him why—surely there were rails in and out of the town, being that it contained a large ironworks facility? The colored man just shook his head and crossed his arms over his chest.

"No," he said, "not anymore, sir. That town's been cut off for years, since the ironworks closed down. They tore up the rails and no one goes there anymore. I'm not even so sure there's anybody living there today."

Roman isn't one to show emotions like other people, at least not strong emotions. But he hung his head and clenched his fists at the words, the frustration rolling off of him. "Where is it?" he asked Butters, but not looking up again.

The ex-conductor sighed heavily and told him Jordan was at least a hundred miles from Horton Corners, and on the other side of a mountain range. I could have struck the man at his next words: "You're not going there any time soon, sir."

That was it then, I thought. We knew *where* we had to go, and Roman knew *what* to do once we got there, but we had no *way* to get there…or at least, as Butters had so damnably put it, any time soon.

Roman unclenched his fists and was standing right in front of the ex-conductor before I had even drawn another breath. He reached out, took the man by the shoulders, and demanded he tell him whatever else it was he wasn't saying. A young life hung by a thread, and it would be on his conscience if he withheld anything that could prevent her death. Butter looked at Roman numbly, not speaking at first, and I almost thought he might be possessed as Clowers had been, but then he started mumbling something. I tried to hear it, but even straining my ears I couldn't. Roman, though, leaned in and turned his ear to the man's lips.

"What?" he asked, standing up straight again. "What does that mean?"

"No, sir," said Butters, a look of defiance come into his eyes. "No, sir. It doesn't mean a thing."

From there, Roman found a chair and fell into a kind of stupor that lasted for hours. He was defeated. Whatever he'd heard from Butters flummoxed him…and Roman Janus is not the kind of man you easily flummox. I took a chair myself and drifted off into an uneasy sleep, not knowing what to do and feeling very, very defeated myself.

At some later hour—well, actually just about thirty minutes ago, Roman rose from his chair, said, "Of course, of course…" and grab-

bing his coat ran out the door without another word.
Now he's back and telling me he's sent a telegram to Joshua.

Valerie

MOUNT AIRY, TROUGHTON HOUSE

TO: ROMAN JANUS
LILAC INN, HORTON CORNERS, COUNTY PETER

SIR,

MUCH TOO LONG TO SEND BOOK IF SITUATION
MOST URGENT AS YOU SAY. AM RISING UP FROM MY
TIN ROOF BLUES TO BRING IT MYSELF. STAY PUT,
HELP ON THE WAY.

JOSHUA

Dear Diary,

Joshua is here.

The man drove day and night from Mount Airy, for nearly twenty-four hours, to reach us here in Horton Corners…but, of course, Dear One, you don't know Joshua Hargreaves.

Joshua is—what is he? A fan of jazz, a writer, and now supposedly a ghost-hunter. I have little personal history with him, save for the time I had him arrested for the murder of Roman and brought to trial. That, as is said, is another story entirely and one Joshua himself has already told in his infamous bestseller. I haven't read it myself, being as I was there, in and out, for much of it. His wife Wendy is an old friend of my family's, a nice girl who for some reason has agreed to put up with Joshua's itinerant behavior.

Roman and Joshua have an odd connection, one I don't fully understand. Today, when they saw each other, they paused and then embraced. Even still, there's an awkwardness between them for which I haven't quite divined the reason.

Regardless, while Joshua drove like a madman over hill and dale with Roman's book, my companion paced the floors almost constantly while I tended to Laura. Roman had me fetch some certain herbs from a nearby market I'd found, and concoct a tincture that he says has helped sustain her body while her soul remains constrained elsewhere. Her father has begun to wake from his stupor—Roman says possession is not a thing to be undergone lightly, and takes its toll on the host. That and Chase stands as one of the strongest spirits ever to roam the Earth, allegedly.

We have attempted to explain what's happened to Clowers, but though he nods his head at what we've told him, I feel he doesn't fully comprehend it yet.

Roman has also plied Butters for answers, but the man has resisted every entreaty to explain himself and what he told Roman.

"I said no such thing," he's insisted, while Roman grows more frustrated with him. He's looked into the Negro's eyes, as he does, and I can tell he knows something else is behind Butters' silence.

And he's told him as much.

"With respect, sir, you don't know anything about it," Butters has replied, "and you shouldn't. It's nothing but trouble. It changes a man."

Roman has pointed out Laura Clowers' dire situation more than once to the ex-conductor, to which he has responded that maybe, just maybe, the girl deserves the harvest she's reaped. I thought I might have to pull my companion off the man after that, but Roman contained himself, to his credit. I myself barely did.

But now Joshua's here, and with him a volume of lore from Roman's precious and extensive library that may illuminate whatever it is that the Spirit-Breaker is seeking. I pray it's so, at least.

Joshua is greeting me now, passing along Wendy's greetings and apologies for not riding along with her husband. She's sick in bed with something, apparently, and I'm almost glad she isn't here to witness this chaos.

Must go now; back when I can.

Valerie

Granny Mima,

I will have to leave the employ of Sgt. Janus. He was good to have offered me a position with him so quickly after the railroad took away mine with them, but the more things happen around him the more I desire to move along. Things happen around him that I have no explanation for.

Somehow, I told him about *wimbo wa treni ya giza*, although that was not my intention. I have no recollection about saying anything about it. If he put a hoodoo on me, I was not aware of it, but it has happened and I cannot take it back. Now he is trying to learn about it despite my warnings. He is a good man, but he will not listen to me. So, I cannot be employed by him.

I also do not care for the way the woman looks at me. She watches me sometimes as if I've done something wrong.

Granny Mima, I did not go to school to be treated like this. I did not learn to read and write, something you were never taught to do, to be treated like this. I did not work for twenty years for the railroad to be set aside like this. I will not wear chains as you did. I will be my own man as I have for many years now.

I don't want to be involved in the things Sgt. Janus gets into. No one should. I cannot be responsible for these people and the things that happen to them because they look into and learn things they shouldn't. I won't help them any further.

But something has compelled me to…and it frightens me.

Gabriel

...at this point in the two men's journey across the continent, they left the shreds of the modern world behind to enter into the Old World, a singular landscape of which they possessed little knowledge and even less patience. The evidence of their frustration with their surroundings became manifest as they traveled deeper into them, according to Helvie, their man-at-arms and ersatz guide.

The small native village they had departed on the morning of 10 September, 1844, receded in the men's memories, nearly completely forgotten, save for the elderly cleric or priest—a description with which neither would later be satisfied—who continued his queer murmurings throughout their last night in the place and onto day-break. It was thought of as a kind of song or chant, as Bowen report-ed it, and at times while they cut through brush and bough it came to mind. Helvie even caught both men humming what he believed to be the exact melody. In all, he could not explain it rationally.

Following a slow trek up a hillside they surmounted on the first day away from the village, the party made camp in the shadows of a stand of tall trees, some of them boasting of girths exceeding seven to eight feet. It was there that the first of a series of inexplicably odd occurrences began to plague the men.

Firstly, Helvie experienced rapid palpitations of his heart mus-cles, a condition he initially attributed to the water the men had filled their canteens with at the village spring, but lasted only for a few minutes until the man sat down and remained immobile while the heart activity returned to normal.

After that, both Bowen and Bowdling found themselves unable to speak for nearly thirty minutes, a situation which caused some distress, but as it passed they came to credit it to exhaustion brought about by their march and the unpacking of their camp. Helvie, who had not yet told the men of his heart condition at that time, grew concerned over the coincidence of all three of them experiencing temporary disabilities. Once he calmed himself, though, the most quizzical of the occurrences manifested.

While the party ate a light supper and the sun was setting, each one of the men in turn exclaimed out loud that they were experiencing the oddest sensation they'd ever come under in their lives. Comparing notes in its aftermath, they decided amongst themselves that it was a very particular and unsettling feeling of something invisible and unseen passing through their bodies.

Bowen had come from good stock and held several degrees in various disciplines; Bowdling's life-story was much the same. Though Helvie hadn't the extensive education of the two men, he'd been living on the continent for close to twenty-nine years in 1844 and had gained a kind of thorough schooling from his experiences there—none of the three could be said to be men of weak character or prone to exaggeration and embroidering of their encounters. The event involved a trio of trustworthy sources with sterling reputations to uphold.

For the most part, sleep was said to have eluded the party that night, though each of the men talked the next morning of strange dreams. Upon comparison, their stories once again jibed; they all witnessed a dark shape of a man walking around their camp, humming and mumbling. Helvie then committed to a thorough search of the camp's grounds and surroundings, but found no evidence whatsoever of any human activity besides his own and that of Bowen and Bowdling. In a way, this came as a relief to all three as the local populace struck them, especially the two older men, as a disagreeable lot, primitive and prone to superstition and embracing barbarism. They had set out without bearers from among the native peoples, believing themselves perfectly adequate in traversing the land with only Helvie's assistance. Dark dreams aside, their journey into the jungle had been relatively easy up to this point, and sans evidence of any native annoyances they foresaw little reason to doubt they would complete it with any more queer happenings.

Yet, it was not to be. The party struck out again with the rising of the sun and almost immediately began to once more encounter what they came to see as resistance from the landscape, its flora and fauna, all around them.

The jungle appeared to press in on them as they walked, and Bowdling claimed he felt like he was being watched at all times.

Bowen and Helvie swore they'd been touched on their arms and necks, almost as if by fingers, but saw no insects or other flying creatures that could account for the sensation. The prolonged exposure to the phenomena wore on each of them, and their irritation with each other and their trek grew into outright arguments and suspicions. Helvie would later note that he quite seriously considered leaving the other two men to their own devices and abandon them in the jungle on more than one occasion as the hours progressed that day. When they realized they were approaching their ultimate destination, he nearly cried out with vocal relief, despite his years of experience in the area.

When the falls were finally in sight, the party rushed forward as one body to enter the clearing and approach the marvel of nature Bowen and Bowlding had heard of and felt moved to see with their own eyes. What awaited them there, though, would forever cloud their memories of the journey and its destination. As they walked to the pool that lie at the base of the falls, they saw a figure standing by its edge as if waiting for them to arrive.

Helvie recognized the figure first and informed his charges that it was the elderly priest from the village they'd left a few days before. The native stood there by the pool with a small smile on his face, his entire body serene and calm, and though his lips were sealed the same odd humming issued from them as they heard the day they departed the village. Helvie indicated this to the others, but both men denied they remembered it. In addition to this strange sight, they all could see a tiny encampment only a few feet away from the priest, of which the remains of its fire was noted by the guide to be at least a day old, if not somewhat older. In all, it was apparent that the small man had been at the falls for more than twenty-four hours, flying in the face of all reason as the white men could see it.

The native continued to stare at them, but after a moment opened his mouth to speak the words *wimbo wateri ya giza*, and *wimbo wa giza wa gri moshi*. This is as Helvie reported it, as close to a faithful transcription as he could determine from only hearing it said once. The man had unfortunately never truly learned the native language of the area, and did not recognize the phrases as anything he'd ever heard before from the primitive peoples who occupied the land. The priest intoned them with a smile, looking from man to man to man as he did. This enraged the party and they thought to rush the small figure to make him account for the impossible thoughts that overwhelmed them, but as they took their first steps toward the priest a great wind arose, seemingly from nowhere, and nearly swept all three from their feet. The native appeared wholly unmoved by the gale and merely stood his ground, still smiling.

Bowen and Bowlding felt diminished by the occurrence, and despite their arduous trek they told Helvie they wished to leave the falls and make for their original starting point on the coast. The guide informed them they'd need to go through the native village again, and after some debate on the point it was decided it was a necessary evil. Passing through the spot, they did not linger as their apprehension of seeing the priest once more move from place to place without impediment from the landscape, and with great speed, was far too much for them to bear.

To this day, the event has defied explanation, and in addition, the priest's words have never truly been deciphered to any knowledgeable expert's satisfaction.

From there, Bowen and Bowdling traveled to...

Excerpt from "Africa" in *Portus Tempestate*
By Jonas Svergaard
Published in 1889 by Ferrer, Straus, and Gimble

Dear Diary,

I write this to you as I sit in a chair at the train station, gazing out into the darkness at a lonely, unused track. It is nearly midnight, and I find myself wide awake, brimming with fear, apprehension, dread, and worry. As my father might have said, "It's a blasted fine way to be when a person ought to be in his bed."

Roman has asked me, actually asked me, to document the next several minutes of this "adventure." I say that in the most mocking, facetious way possible. This may be an adventure to, say, the likes of Joshua, but I have had my fill of it. And why shouldn't I? The matter has been taken out of my hands entirely by my companion. Roman is leaving, and I am staying.

"It's about the singing, isn't it?" he asked Gabriel Butters once he'd finished reading a long passage from the book Joshua brought him from his library in Janus House. "My Swahili is very poor, but I think I get the gist of it. It's about a kind of a pathway."

Butters replied sourly, "It's the Dark Walk, sir, and it's not for you." To which Roman commented in his matter-of-fact way, "I suppose this time we'd better call it the Dark Track."

I'm not sure what was worse, my argument with Roman or his with Butters. I won't detail mine, save to say I presented my case about going with him to Jordan—Roman is certain he has the way there, and quickly—but he wouldn't hear of it and now, after twice explaining to me what he is doing, refuses to listen to my entreaties. He *can* be a stubborn man when he wants to be. With Butters, the debate was purely about Roman's plan, no matter who it was who was going.

"I've told you, sir," he said to my companion, "it changes a man. I once caught a glimpse of it when I was a younger man and among people who knew about these things, and I can tell you it's nothing that anyone should be part of."

Roman persisted. "You can help that girl. You can help me save that girl. I need to get to that town and I can't see any other way there." He paused, and then: "And I *do* know of such things... though I admit I didn't know of this one, not until I remembered a

79

passage in a book, at least. I recently told a large group of, well, my people, I suppose, to be *open to that which we do not already know. To be open to larger things.* I intend to honor that tonight."

Butters grew surlier. "A few words in a book doesn't—don't mean you *know* about this, sir. I won't be party to it. I won't have it on my conscience, no matter how sick the girl is."

That's the long and short of it, Dear One. There was more, but it amounted to a carousel, the two of them going 'round and 'round it until they finally ceased and went their separate ways. As Roman and I have done, too, I guess. But I *am* chronicling it, as he asked.

That brings us up to the here and now. I am writing this as it happens.

Roman has walked out onto the track. We are the only ones in this area of the yard: Roman, myself, Joshua, Butters, and Daniel Clowers. Roman is now facing to the west and has raised his arms, a bit more than horizontally. He is…my Lord, he's singing.

Joshua beside me has pricked up his ears, listening. He says it's the "Carrollton March"… the very first train song. I am telling Joshua to be quiet—Roman, bless him, has a very poor singing voice. But the way it's moving around, echoing. Why is it echoing like that?

Butters is frowning heavily, but remaining silent. Clowers is also frowning, but I'll give him that. It's more than he's done in days.

Something is happening. Oh, I hear…*I hear a train.*

Joshua just confirmed it's not from one of the other tracks, the tracks that are actually used by the station. No, this is far off, but—wait. Roman is closing his eyes, he's stopped singing. He's moving his arms out in front of him, palms turned to the west…he's concentrating on something.

The train is coming. I can see it now.

Butters is shifting back and forth now, behind me. My God, if he does anything to interrupt Roman, I will… oh, the train. It's there. Right there. Roman is right in its path!

I am back on my chair now. My heart is beating wildly, but I'm telling myself it's okay. The train is here. I don't know how, but it's right here, and we can all see it. Roman is singing again, but softly, and walking now towards the train, past its engine and…the thing is—what is it? Smoky, but I smell no smoke. I mean it looks smoky, and like a locomotive from when I was a girl. Like the ones that went past my father's fort.

No, wait. It's changed. It looks like a drawing of a train I saw, the early ones. The *earliest* ones. And now…it's changing again. I don't know what I'm looking at.

Joshua is agog, as is Clowers. Butters…I don't see him. I don't know where he's gone to. Roman is now walking alongside one of the cars, looking up at it. He's stopping, looking…oh! There is someone on the train. It appears to be a conductor.

Roman is stepping over to the steps up to the car. Oh! I just called out to him to be careful, but he didn't hear me? Can he hear me? The car doesn't look solid—he'll fall if he tries to mount the steps…

The conductor has no face, or no face I can see. Where it should be is smoke. The man's hand is reaching out, palm up…Lord, I think he's asking Roman for a ticket. Roman is staring at him, reaching into his own pocket for…he's uncertain; I can see that. But, there's a ticket! It was in Roman's pocket! He's glanced at it—now handing it up to the conductor. The man is taking it, looking at it, nodding.

Roman is turning his head, looking at me, giving me a short, military nod. I'm crying. I'm sorry, but I'm crying.

Singing. I hear singing. It's…Butters? He is singing:

"Roll, Jordan, roll
We march the angel march"

The conductor is reaching out his hand again, but to Butters, who is walking slowly, hesitantly toward the train. Now he's reaching in his pocket—he has a ticket, too. Why? Why would he do this when all along he's denied Roman the—he's given the ticket to the conductor. Roman has put his hand on Butters' shoulder and is giving him a nod, too, as if to say he agrees?

No! I have just told Joshua to stay put! He stepped toward the train saying he knows quite a few jazz tunes about trains—Good

Lord, I need him here. They can't all ride this—*this train to Hell*. I need him here to help me take care of the Clowers.

No. No, no, no…the conductor is looking at *me*.

I find I can write, at least. I can barely speak, but I can write. Oh, Dearest Diary, I am on the train. *I am on the train.*

There was a ticket in my pocket. It wasn't there before. Did I sing? Was I singing along with Roman and didn't know it? I don't know that song he sang…I feel confused. And very, very frightened. The car is…changing. One moment it's of our own time, and then it's…old? No, it looks modern, but wait…there are people ahead of us, sitting there, oh God, don't let them turn around.

They are *smoke*. Everything is *smoke*.

Roman is beside me—no, he's gotten up! Oh, Lord, what is he doing? I can't move, I can only write, though my hands are cold, my fingers going numb. Butters. Where is Butters? Where is Roman?

I have to get up. Still writing? What is—

Part Two

THE DARK TRACK

Spring

QUIGGLEY'S GHOST

April 20

Today is the first day of spring, and as good a day as any to take up my writing again.

It has been nearly a year since Robert has been gone, almost twelve full months since the Accident. The house is quite literally a shrine to him, but I need to get up and out of it and find work. I can no longer lean on my neighbors for charity. My soul won't have it.

It has been more than seven years since we came to this place together; Robert to help build the dam that has made this little valley a home for many, and me to support him in sickness and in health, 'til death do us part. It has been six years since he decided to stay on and go to work for the Jordan Ironworks and Mr. Russell Jordan, the man who had the dam built and this town not long after. It was quite an adventure for a while, but our lives became stable and rote, but I never complained. I was with Robert and that was all I wanted.

I still wore black until today. Today I laid aside my bombazine and crepe and my jewelry of deepest jet to risk public censure, the widow who wouldn't wait the proper time to stop mourning her husband. But, as I said, I needed to find work. My soul needed to find work.

Yesterday I sat and thought about what I could do. The list included cooking and baking, sewing and mending, and tending to the sick and elderly. None of those appealed to me, though, so I settled upon—and I find this remarkable—watching children. From where deep down inside of me that arose I have no idea, as Robert and I had no children of our own, but it suits me, and so I have already found my first charges. I will spend the day with my neighbor's two sons, Uly and Michael Soames, and give their ailing mother the peace and quiet she needs to heal from her long illness.

I collected the two boys at ten o'clock this morning and asked them where they would like to go for an outing. The older of them, Uly, noticed my bright, spring dress and gave me a momentary look—his father is the minister at our little church—but when little Michael began to note his choices the elder brother voiced his own preferences in louder fashion. He surprised me by saying he should like to walk past the Negroes in their shanty town in the south part of Jordan, but I told him that would be a thoroughly disreputable thing for the sons of a minister to do. Uly didn't care for that much, but he asserted himself once more over Michael's suggestions of the park or the hog pen out by the smokehouse and said he would very much like to visit the train station.

I saw no reason why the station wouldn't be a suitable destination for us. Michael, though, found it cause to begin crying, and when I asked him why such a thing would upset him, he told me the station frightened him. I assured him there was nothing there that should frighten him, and if there was that I would be with him the entire time, as well as his older brother. This seemed to mollify him and so we struck out on our walk.

The outside air was breezy and a bit chilly with the last dregs of winter still hanging about, but the sun was out, bright and cheerful, and it made for a pleasant ramble through Jordan on our way to the station. Our little valley spread out before us, I enjoyed being out and about with a purpose, and despite a few glances of surprise from certain neighbors and other townsfolk as to my dress and its lack of a somber tone, I began to enjoy myself.

After passing the temperance hall and the church, we waved at the blacksmith and wished him a good day. As we approached the Ironworks, Uly suggested we look in on the carpentry shop there, but I kept us moving and the thought passed quickly without debate. The Jordan Ironworks is a massive place, dominating the town with its scope and size, as well it should. There would be no such place as Jordan if not for it. We soon passed the great forge building, the water tower, and the coal sheds, and to my relief the sight of it all did not bring me to tears. In fact, a sense of pride in Robert grew within my breast as I reflected on his good works for the company over the years, a feeling that magnified when off in the distance beyond the Ironworks we caught a glimpse of the dam that he helped build.

Finally passing beyond the Ironworks, we came to the House on the Hill, the home of Mr. Russell Jordan himself. Uly thought that perhaps we might see the great man standing on his porch and look-ing over his town, but I reminded the boy that Mr. Jordan hadn't appeared outside his home for almost five years, and there would be little chance of it. As we walked on, I couldn't help but feel the House on the Hill still wore a note of sadness about it, even after all these years.

The train station is, of course, for passenger travel, not the sprawl-ing web of tracks that services the Ironworks. Our small station can be an exciting place for young children to visit, and I was glad to see a train having just pulled into it as we arrived there. Michael was hesitant to enter, but once inside his grip on my hand loosened somewhat and he looked all around at the activity. I noted a group of Negroes, a family I presumed waiting for someone to disembark, and thought Uly would be pleased to have gotten his original wish. The group greeted a Negro from the train, a man who I suppose would be considered handsome among his kind, albeit a bit portly.

As I turned to say something to Uly, it was then I saw that little Michael's nose was bleeding. Tamping down inwardly on any panic, I knelt down with a handkerchief from my clutch and dabbed at the small trickle of crimson while Uly groaned at what he saw as some sort of betrayal by his younger sibling. Screwing up my courage, I informed both boys we couldn't stay if Michael's nose continued to bleed, and so with a promise we'd return to the station in a few days we exited almost as soon as we'd arrived, Uly complaining all the way. We spent the remainder of the day at the park, and yes, looking at the hogs. Michael, the bleeding finally stopped, was very happy at the day's outcome, while his brother was certain the younger So-ames had somehow engineered the nosebleed to thwart any sort of fun Uly was owed.

I offered my thoughts on the boy's grand imagination as we headed home, but kept my counsel on the oddness of the event—Michael wasn't prone to such, so far as I knew. Regardless, I invited the boys to come to my house to help me make a nice supper for their parents, but they declined and I spent the next few hours cook-ing in my kitchen, glad to be on the road to self-sufficiency at last.

May 4

Two weeks have passed since I took the Soames boys to the train station, and in that time it has rained almost incessantly. Finally, today offered some cease in hostilities and I extended my invitation to the brothers for another try. Uly was more than pleased to accept, but Michael wasn't feeling well and stayed home to be doted on by his mother.

The station seemed busier today than during our ill-fated visit of two weeks ago, with a train sitting on the tracks there, disgorging passengers, and another that pulled in after we'd been there a short while. I marveled at how our small town had become so desirable, knowing full well the reasons for most of the arrivals were most likely terribly mundane. Still, the day was pleasant, Uly was behaving himself, and I was in good spirits myself. We spent a good hour there, reading the train schedules, looking over the great map of the country with its railroads clearly marked, treating ourselves to a strawberry ice from a vendor's cart, and watching the people come and go. Uly appeared fascinated by it all, and I suggested he might want to consider a position on the railway in his future.

As we were preparing to leave and head home again, I noticed a disembarking passenger who caught my eye. He was handsome in a rugged way, with close-cropped sandy hair and no beard, as well as a dark patch he wore over his right eye. It was perhaps his garb that stood out the most, pants and tunic made from what I guessed to be worked leather, an old rucksack strung over his chest with a broad strap, and high boots that desperately needed some attention. I wondered if he might be a war veteran, an unfortunate who lost an eye during a battle or some such. His hands were clean enough, though, and showed little signs of soldiering or any other hard work, but there were lines in his face that I believed told a tale or two of his hardships.

It was when I realized Uly was pulling at my arm that I recognized what I'd been doing: staring at the man and observing him to the point of pausing in my crossing the station to exit it. The boy was oblivious to the situation, thankfully, and I shook off my reverie to urge him to continue on our way. The last thing I noticed was the man being greeted by another man who had stepped up to him with an extended hand of welcome. Just as Uly and I were passing through the doorway to the outside, the identity of the second man came to mind: one of the foremen at the Jordan Ironworks, someone I had met before through Robert. It made some sense to me then, as I imagined the newly arrived man had come to Jordan seeking employment at the Ironworks and was already being taken in hand by his new employer.

Yes, that sounded entirely reasonable I thought as Uly and I walked home. His mother was up and about the house, fully re-covered and eager to talk gossip with me. I begged her forgiveness for not staying, claiming I had a headache. Mrs. Soames never does seem to realize I rarely indulge her in gossiping, especially concern-ing her favorite subject, the Jordan family. I believe she thinks I am somehow close with them, but in truth beyond a dinner Robert and I once attended at the House on the Hill and a very brief time when I entertained his daughter, I have little to say about the matter. Still, she tries to engage me on it nearly every time I see her.

How queer it is that I continue to think about the man in the train station even now as I sit here this evening with my writing.

May 9

I saw him again, the man from the station, the one the eyepatch and the odd clothes. I had walked to our little grocer's in town to purchase a few things I needed for a pie, and after being there only a minute or two he stepped in and almost immediately our eyes met. It was purely happenstance as I was already looking toward the door momentarily, but regardless I turned away immediately out of propriety. Whether or not he did, also, I cannot say for sure, but before I knew it he was only a few inches from me and begging my pardon.

I have not spoken to any unmarried man—I assume he is unmarried, for he wears no wedding band—since Robert died, and did not care to take up the habit today. Though I no longer wear black I am in no mood to converse with any man save the postmaster, the blacksmith, the grocer, and any other married individual I encounter in everyday life. His presence unnerved me somehow, and his close proximity weighed heavily upon me for some reason. Inwardly I prayed someone who knew me and my status would speak up and save me from an unpleasant scene.

Instead, the man introduced himself as James. I amazed myself by asking him in return if that was his surname or Christian name. He smiled slightly, dipped his head, and replied that his full name was Roland James. Then, he added that he wanted me to know that Robert was always with me, and was in fact with me at that very moment.

I began to cry. Or, as Robert might have said, I "went all to pieces." Somehow, I made my way back outside the grocer's so as to remove myself from the situation—and more importantly from the man's presence. It was all a blur to me; one moment I was gazing at strawberries, the next a strange man was telling me my late husband was supposedly standing there with me…and how he knew Robert's name I will never know.

Someone checked on me, I forget who, but I told them I was fine and walked away to place some distance between myself and the building. And that man. As I walked I pondered solutions to the questions that had arisen: Could someone have arranged the event, perhaps a kind of joke? Was I to be the victim of some sort of flummery? Jordan is small, or at least compared to other towns, and very insular. We all know each other, more or less; who would be so cruel to play such a trick on me concerning Robert?

The park beckoned to me, a refuge or a port in a storm. I took a bench off to one side of the little, green area and tried to focus on the birds gathered about on the grass. I had been there only ten minutes or so when a shadow eclipsed my sight and I looked up to see that man again, standing there looking down on me with his single eye— which I noticed was a peculiar color, hard to define.

This man, this Roland James, begged my pardon for the second time and asked if he could sit down and talk to me. I sprung up from the bench and was about to tell him in no uncertain terms that the bench would be entirely his, for I would be gone from the park within seconds. But then something changed in me. There was something about him I couldn't identify, a quality or...well, I faced him and instead told him to speak his piece, and quickly.

"I need Robert's help." That's what he said; just that. I felt faint, but held on and informed him how difficult that would be considering my husband's death several months ago. The man held my gaze, seemingly unperturbed by my words and tone, and after a moment of silence told me he knew very well Robert's state, but needed his help regardless.

I looked all around, at the park, the trees, the people enjoying their day, and when I looked back at Mr. James I took a deep breath and, very calmly, asked him what he meant by that. He smiled the same smile he'd offered at the grocer's, one that was equal parts friendliness, tolerance, and knowledge. Then, he waved his hand to the bench and begged me to sit and listen to his story. Amazing myself once more, I sat.

Roland James was called to Jordan by the head of the entire Jordan Ironworks—to rid the place of a spirit. A ghost, that is. A spook or specter, one of those wretched souls we read about in Dickens tales...and the man who sat on the bench with me was someone who could allegedly drive such a creature off. Setting that revelation aside for the moment, I inquired as to whom the Jordan Ironworks spirit might be, and what my late husband had to do with it. No sooner than the words had left my lips it dawned on me what Mr. James might be getting at, and I reared back, my hand rising to slap the insult right off his face. Sensing this, apparently, he quickly threw up his hands to ask my forgiveness and assure me he did *not* mean at all that Robert was haunting the Ironworks. No, but it was someone who my husband knew…in life.

My head swam, and I told the man, the ghost-hunter, I would need a moment to digest it all. I could see he understood completely, perhaps having encountered such reactions to his proclamations as to the spirit-world before, and sat silently while I composed myself. Once I was squared away again, I asked him to continue, not wanting to admit that a part of me was both engaged and intrigued by the story.

When he was done, I learned that a man everyone knew as Quiggley was the spectral culprit in question. Memories washed over me of the elderly ironworker, a cantankerous soul who came along from the previous Jordan works to the new town and settled right back into his role as someone you both feared and admired. Robert somehow won Quiggley's respect and became one of the few fellow employees the old man would even speak to with anything resembling a neutral tone. This lasted more than a year before Quiggley was found one afternoon in his work spot, the apparent victim of a heart attack. The Jordan Ironworks quickly forgot him, but Robert held onto his respect for him and spoke of him to me long after he was dead and buried.

And now, according to Mr. James, Quiggley was causing quite a ruckus at the forge. I asked again what Robert had to do with it, if it were even true to begin with, and the answer I received was that my husband, being the old man's only real friend at the Ironworks, could mollify him and allow the ghost-hunter to send the spirit on his way to his ultimate reward. I tried to speak, to ask a thousand questions, but I could only stutter my reply until I calmed myself once again and forced some composure into my blood.

I was told then that Robert is always with me, providing Mr. James with a pathway to my husband, and subsequently to Quiggley. It was more than I could bear, apparently, for the next thing I knew I awoke in Mrs. Soames' bedroom with the news that I had fainted in the park...and that the "nice gentleman" who had come to my rescue would be calling on me tomorrow to see that I was all right.

May 11

Roland James did not appear the next day as I was told he would, but in a way I was relieved, for it gave me time to think about everything he'd spoken to me about. And when I did go over it all in my mind, I found it sat easier there than the day before. In short, I don't know why it surprised and bothered me then, for today I see that it's actually quite interesting.

If there is life of a kind beyond the grave, some way for our souls to survive the great journey and linger here on Earth, I would like to think of Robert as near me and watching over me. That in itself is a comfort. The idea of vengeful ghosts, or even vexing ones, is not, and that coupled with what I suppose I looked upon as the impropriety of a stranger inquiring as to personal matters from a widow was what affected me before. But today? Strangely, it doesn't have the same impact anymore. I feel as if I could hear more about it from Mr. James and wondered if he would still call on me.

So, yesterday while I waited I went about my normal tasks, but all the while I conjured up memories of Quiggley and the very few times I met him as well as the very many times Robert talked about him. Those occasions made me feel as if I knew the man and could see what Robert saw in him—a man who gave his life for a company, and who felt as if no one else around him understood the sacrifices he'd made in that pursuit. Somehow, as I've said, my husband struck a chord in Quiggley, and supposedly that was what Mr. James needed to go about his business of chasing away spirits.

Looking back over what I've just written, it seems so absurd, yet also…familiar?

But how could that be? The feeling intensified when earlier today there came a knock at my door and I opened it to find Roland James standing there smiling and asking me if I'd considered his request. I told him yes, I would try to have Robert help him, but I was completely adrift about such things—how would I know how to do that? Mr. James said firstly, may he come in to talk with me? That was out of the question, I returned; though a widow, I held a good standing in the community and had no desire to sully it by inviting a man into my house without anyone else present. He offered the idea of walking to the park where we talked the other day. That was agreeable to me, and so I acquired a wrap and a hat and we were on our way. Perhaps it wasn't much less shocking to be seen outdoors with him as to be seen taking him into my home, but at that moment my concern over it was slipping away.

As we walked, I studied his face. It was a good face, though rough around the edges, and I noticed the patch over his eye was much thicker than I'd realized. Gathering my courage, I asked him if he'd been a soldier. His reply came after a long pause, one in which the man appeared at odds with himself over how to answer. Shortly though, he told me he wasn't sure of his past status, as he'd been an amnesiac for some years, and in fact was still—he had no real idea what he'd been in life before just a few years ago. One day, he opened his eyes and saw spirits around him, or what he believed to be spirits, and found that he could influence their behavior. Within a very short time, he discovered he could actually drive them off and spare we living, breathing souls the onus of their presence.

I considered his words and again found I wasn't scandalized by them, nor did I fully invest in them, either. It was all very difficult to credit. Thankfully, before Mr. James could ask me what I thought of his situation, the House on the Hill came into view, and he asked me very pointedly what I knew of the Jordans' story. Once more the proposition of gossip confronted me, and so I told him what I knew, but in a way I didn't feel was disgraceful.

Five years ago, I informed Mr. James, Russell Jordan's only child, his daughter Laura, had been abducted from her home. For one week, the man waited for some sort of request for payment to have her returned, but when the letter finally arrived, it told a very different tale. In it, Laura described her kidnapper as a "gentleman" and that not only hadn't he harmed her in any way, but had opened her eyes to many injustices in the world. As she went on, Laura said she wouldn't be returning home, at least not any time soon, and in fact she would be helping the "gentleman" in his pursuits. Once the news got out and the newspapers began to write articles about it, everyone learned her abductor's identity as that of Clement Chase, a notorious criminal with a very long string of offensives across the country. And Laura Jordan, heiress to the Jordan Ironworks fortune, was his accomplice…and presumably still is today, despite any news of a Chase crime for more than a year.

Laura was a good girl—*is* a good girl. I knew her, as I said, for a brief time when Mr. Jordan himself inquired if Robert's wife might be open to watching over his daughter on occasion. That arrangement lasted for roughly two weeks, then ended abruptly. Laura, as I knew her then, was kind and generous, but I could see she was weighed down by the pressure her father placed upon to one day inherit all that he had. Still, the thought she could go along with a criminal, help in his crimes, share his lifestyle, share his…no, it's obscene. Impossible. She's only a girl. *Was* only a girl.

As Mr. James entered the park, I felt immediately at ease again, and found myself walking toward a small pond there that Robert and the local ducks were very fond of. Though I said nothing of this to my companion, he nodded and said it was a wise direction and that Robert would surely agree, almost as if he had read my mind. I let it pass without comment and took a seat on a bench by the pond. Mr. James sat down beside me and we looked out over the water. There was no one else in that section of the park at that time.

"Call out to him, but not with your voice." At first I couldn't comprehend what the man meant, but I mulled the words over and after a moment the meaning seemed to be clear. I thought about Robert. Thought about his face, his hands, his voice, the foods he liked, the way he'd chuckle at my forgetfulness, the way he could become engrossed in the company newspaper. And then, little by little, I believe I caught his scent in the air.

Roland James was forgotten, but then I heard his voice telling me that Robert was closer to me than ever before since he'd died. He didn't have to say anything of the sort, because I *knew* he was. I felt it in my bones, in every bit of me. My husband was there, right there, as surely as if flesh and blood.

"A very loving spirit, indeed," said Mr. James. I saw his words hanging in front of me as if written on a chalkboard. They were not intrusive, as one might imagine they'd be with the sensations I was experiencing, but somehow supportive of them. I wondered if Robert would feel as *there* as he did if not for the man sitting beside me.

"Robert Randolph, I would talk with you, if you'll have it."

From the second Roland spoke those words, it was as if I were in the same room with two men having a conversation, but unable to make out the words. I heard the timbre of my husband's voice, but not exactly what he was saying. The talk went on for several minutes, maybe even longer, but I sat on the bench with my eyes closed and my ears filled with the sound of Robert, and I was content. After a time, his voice faded and I felt a hand on my arm, softly yet also with resolve. I opened my eyes to see Roland smiling at me and telling me Robert had agreed to help him.

And that, as they say, was that. We walked back to my home and I was told he would contact me once he'd "attended to a few matters." With a nod and another smile he was gone.

May 17

Five days have passed since Roland James was here, and there has been no sign of him since. I tried to put the entire experience out of my thoughts for the first few days, but it insinuated itself once again, and I even began to glance out of my windows to see if the man was coming up the walk to rap at my door. But he has not, and I wondered if perhaps I simply imagined the exchange.

Three days ago I walked to the park again, albeit by myself, and sat on the same bench by the same pool. Feeling a bit foolish at first I finally closed my eyes and attempted to conjure up the same feelings I had that day when I was certain Robert had come to me. After a minute or two I realized with a pang in my heart that nothing was happening, or at least nothing so much as the wonderful sensations of that day with Mr. James.

Later, at home again, I tried it again, both sitting in my parlor with the shades drawn and a phonograph record he liked playing and a bit later even in sitting in a warm bath I'd drawn. Still nothing occurred, though I thought I'd caught a fleeting wisp of his scent and that something touched my hair at one point. Frustrated and certain I was working myself into a kind of delusion, I went bed with a promise to put the foolishness behind me.

Yesterday I took myself over to our little Jordan Public Library, and before I knew it I was searching for books on ghosts and spirits. Thankfully, no one I knew was in the building, for I'm not sure what I'd tell them had they spied the material I was reading. Regardless, too much of it was fanciful and amounted to ghost stories of legend and whatnot. I don't doubt that there are some who believe that such things exist in our world, but...

What exactly I'd hoped to find I couldn't say, but the books closed and back on their shelves and my mind clearer and once more rational, I felt myself growing frustrated again—and for nebulous reasons. I left the dusty old tomes behind and made my way home once more, unsure of everything that had happened between myself and Roland James.

Damn the man.

Did he toy with my longing for my husband? Was I duped somehow? And if so, for what purpose? I couldn't see any, at least any that he would gain something from. No, he seemed sincere and kind and he asked my permission, and—

Damn the man. He has to be some sort of charlatan.

But why then do I continue to think about him?

May 20

Two more days passed and I had nearly forgotten all about ghosts and spirits and Roland James. The house needed cleaning—a much-delayed thorough spring cleaning, and I set about the task with relish. It felt very satisfying to open the windows and wipe away the cobwebs, and perhaps even more so to sweep away the little hobgoblins of the mind.

A feeling of dread replaced that of renewal and refreshment, though, when a knock came at my door and I opened it with a distinct sense of déjà vu. Roland James stood there, this time with no smile on his face, but instead an expression of seriousness. He was about something, I could tell. How, I wasn't sure, but he wore it like a cloak, as if he'd come into his own, fully invested in whatever "matters" he'd supposedly been looking into.

"Mrs. Randolph, we're needed," he said, waving his hand to the wider world outside my door. I asked him to clarify that—I was needed? And for what? Inwardly, I had no desire to tell him I'd been watching out my windows for him for days. The serious look melted into a look of confusion; hadn't I been paying attention? he asked. Quiggley, the Ironworks, Robert…had I forgotten? I must go off with him immediately to begin the actual work. Work? What work? And then the confusion was replaced by irritation. *That* didn't look right on him. In fact, it was a bit frightening to see.

I held up both hands to allay his concerns and told him if he could wait an hour I could be ready to accompany him. What a picture I must have been, in my cleaning clothes and head scarf. Confusion returned; an *hour*? he sputtered, disbelieving. Men. Yes, I replied, and it was nothing less than he deserved for popping up out of nowhere on a perfectly normal spring day to interrupt my chores and whisking me away from my home on Heaven-only-knows what kind of an errand. One hour, no less.

One hour later *exactly* and Roland was at my door again. With little to no preamble we were off to the Jordan Ironworks. As we walked he asked me if I had another name he could call me instead of "Mrs. Randolph." Surprised by the question in terms of both cheek and that he didn't already know my first name, I considered the request and the propriety involved, finally allowing him the light intimacy of it. In all, I found I liked the way he said "Marie" when addressing me.

The Ironworks loomed as we approached and I began to craft excuses for our presence. Many of the workers knew me there, comrades of Robert who seemed to enjoy my infrequent visits on my husband's lunchbreaks or even to see him home occasionally. Again, Roland apparently read my mind and assured me he'd been invited to the Ironworks for the very task for which we were headed there, and all was well. I offhandedly mentioned how I'd first seen him in the train station and he nodded matter-of-factly, acting as if he'd known that all along.

I also questioned his continued use of "we" when he spoke of whatever it was he was invited to do. "Marie," he said, glancing at me, "you are my insurance," and left the matter at that. Of course I pressed him to explain that statement, but he would only add that when and if "the time came" I would "know what to do."

If anything, I reasoned to myself, it could make for an amusing afternoon on a typical spring day.

At the gates of the Ironworks, we were met by a sallow-faced man who stepped out of a small shed there and inquired as to our business before he actually looked up at us and appeared to recognize Roland. Then he glanced at me, frowned deeply, and noted the great foundry was "no place for a woman." He was vaguely familiar to me, but I couldn't remember his name; regardless, we were allowed to continue on, and as we approached the main forge, I once more marveled at the great size and power of the works. The heat itself was intense, even at the distance we kept ourselves, and I watched the foundrymen going about their tasks, blessing each one of them and praying their wives would never have to experience what I did with Robert.

Two men broke away from the clutch of workers near a huge vat and walked over to us as they pulled off their thick gloves and wiped sweat from their faces. As they got nearer, I could see I knew them both as friends of Robert's. They seemed cheerful enough as they greeted me and asked how I'd been getting along, but I could also see the underlying shyness and sadness in their demeanors. I was used to it by now; no one knew exactly what to say to me since my husband's death.

There was also a small group of Negroes farther ahead, all talking to one another. They looked up when we approached, but after staring at us for a moment they returned to their discussion. One of them looked familiar to me, but how that would be I don't know.

Roland asked for the foreman on duty, and within a minute Gregory Kane appeared and shook hands with my companion and tipped his cap to me. Ushering us off to a side room, he removed his cap, wiped his face, and became very serious. Roland explained he'd been walking the perimeter of the entire Ironworks the last few days, and that he'd narrowed down his ideas of where to begin to two different spots. Mr. Kane's face held its composure, but I sensed he was not truly a believer in what the ghost-hunter was offering the company. Finally, once the foreman seemed satisfied that we would be fine on our own and would keep our promise to stay clear of the "hot" area of the great forge, he excused himself and went back to his work. Roland turned in place as if getting his bearings and announced that we were to head to the room that contained the workers' lockers.

Memories came flooding back to me of Robert's descriptions of that area and in particular, Quiggley's daily "ritual" there. When we stepped through a door into the room it was almost as if I knew it from personal experience, though of course that would be impossible. It was due to Robert once more; he talked about it so many times I felt I'd been there before. Basically, it was a long row of wooden cabinets with doors all lined up against a wall one after another, and with a long, low wooden bench standing in front of the cabinets. There was a name written in pencil on a small card and attached to the front of each door, most likely ascribed to the workers. Roland didn't hesitate to make his way down the length of the room, his one eye looking across the cabinets as he did. Finally he stopped in front of one, gestured at it, and said, "Here."

When I'd caught up to him I could see the name on the cabinet's card read "Quiggley."

My companion asked me what I was feeling at the moment as we gazed at the door. I shook my head, unsure of what to say, but then I began to tell him about the old man's habit of breaking away each day from his labors at a certain time of the afternoon, not lunchtime or teatime, but somewhere in between, to return to his locker and sit and stare at a certain item he always kept there.

A tintype, Roland said, of a young woman and a baby. I nodded in agreement; just as Robert told me. No one knew who the two in the photograph were, and no one dared ask the old man. It seemed to be from many years before, and in poor condition, as if it had been carried from place to place in a pocket, folded and crumpled many times over. Quiggley would stare at it for fifteen minutes or so, and then return to his work without a word. He was never chastised for the behavior by the foremen, and he never offered any excuses or explanation for the ritual. It just was, and everyone at the Jordan Ironworks accepted it.

Roland asked me if I felt anything else, or if any other stories came to mind. I admitted that nothing else occurred to me, but I felt a bit tired and sat down on the bench. After a moment, he sat down beside me and we both stared at the cabinet together.

The lights went out then.

Darkness rushed in, so deep I couldn't see my hand in front of my face. Old fears not felt since childhood assailed me, and my confidence melted away. I gasped and reached out for Roland, my fingers brushing his arm and clutching at the fabric of his sleeve. My other hand went to my face to muffle my panic as I heard him speak to me as if he were being carried off from the bench, his voice distorted and weakening: "Marie! Stay where you are!"

Somehow, I obeyed, though my heart pounded in my chest and I began to sob. I felt suddenly icy cold as a chilly breeze swept up and over me—I knew in a flash that the cabinet door in front of me had swung open and I gripped Roland's arm even tighter.

Though he sat right next me, his presence heavy and real, Roland's voice sounded even farther away than before when he told me to call out to my husband.

"Robert!" I shouted, breaking off from my sobbing. My own voice seemed strange to me, alien and unreal. "Robert!" I cried again as tears ran down my face into my lap. I prayed that the lights would come back on, as I had never experienced darkness so deep and thick.

With growing alarm, I realized Robert was not coming to my aid. Why would I have ever thought that in the first place? There was something about Roland James that inspired such a belief. That and his arm as an anchor. I screamed my husband's name again, but my cry only echoed around in the darkness of the room.

Something scraped across wood and fell to the floor with a crash. It must be something in the cabinet, I thought, and resisted the urge to lean down and feel around for whatever it was. Roland again read my mind and demanded I stay perfectly still. I told him I was trying, but it was so hard. I begged him not to make me let go of his arm.

"Marie," he said, his voice shot through with surprise, "I'm nowhere near you."

Perhaps another person in my place would have released their hand from the position it was in. Another person would have opened their fingers and taken back their hand from whoever's sleeve they'd been gripping like a vice. That person was not me; in fact, my own hand was locked in that grip, and a scream to shake the walls of the room was building up inside of me, quivering for release.

Someone whispered—no, *hissed*—in my ear: "Go away!"

I swooned and fell across the bench. When I opened my eyes, the room was lit up once again and Roland was kneeling down beside me, patting my hand. Together as one, we looked at it and saw it was covered in soot and ashes.

Then, there on the floor in front of the open cabinet with the name of Quiggley on it, was a severely warped tintype of a young woman and a smiling child.

May 21

I slept fitfully last night after storming home following the harrowing experience at the Ironworks. I had refused to listen to Roland James' explanations of why he'd gotten up from the bench without saying anything to me—he'd flown over to the door to find it locked—and why he didn't return to the bench—he was afraid of scaring Quiggley off. I walked home alone, practically in a daze, and shut myself up for the evening.

This morning I rose from my bed feeling miserable, irritable and angry. Thoughts roiled within me, so much so that I completely abandoned the cleaning I had begun yesterday to pace the floor and curse the name of my erstwhile companion.

Had he planned it all along? Was it a kind of a joke? Or were we truly in the presence of something not easily explained and he'd placed me there with little thought of how I might react to it?

Why, oh why did I do it? I asked myself. Was I so easily gulled? Were all the women he approached as charmed as I was? I fumed and fretted all morning, and with each question I grew angrier. When he came to call again at my door, as I knew he would, I felt I was ready for him, ready to give him a good piece of my mind and then shut him out of my life forever.

I opened the door to look at his contrite expression, but didn't give him a chance to speak. Rather, I ordered him to come in. He quietly asked me what the neighbors might think, etc. "Blast the neighbors!" I told him and gestured for him to enter. Once inside the door I stopped him in the foyer and steeled myself for the onslaught. What was it all about? I demanded. Was it just to make a fool of me at my late husband's place of work? Why else did he insist I go along with him to the Ironworks?

Taking a deep breath, he let it out and pierced me through with his one good eye.

He said he had spent many hours and days to determine Robert was necessary to pacifying Quiggley's spirit, and that my presence would help my husband "come through" even stronger. Furthermore, he explained that he didn't know why it all happened as it did, and why Robert didn't manifest. Quiggley had seen something in Robert, something that made him trust him over anyone else at the Ironworks, and it might have had something to do with the photograph of the woman and child. He wasn't certain on that score.

I reacted very poorly to that supposition, feeling that somehow he was insinuating my husband was involved in some manner with the woman. Harsh words flowed from my mouth, a steady stream of accusations intended to show I did not appreciate such suggestions.

Then, all at once, Roland held up a hand, looked around the room, and said he felt something was very, very wrong in my house.

This alarmed me, of course, but suspicion replaced that emotion almost immediately until I swore I heard something move in the parlor, not ten feet or so from where we were standing. There wasn't any way for the man to have made the sound from where he stood, unless he was a magician of some kind. I started to protest, but just then a picture suddenly flew off its hook on the wall and nearly hit Roland in the shoulder.

"Quickly!" he shouted. "Clear a table, Marie!"

The request was strange to me and I froze in place, unsure of what he meant. He didn't waste a second and stepped over to the small table in the middle of the parlor and swept it clean of its centerpiece and coverlet. Then, motioning to a chair standing next to it, he commanded me to sit in it. I obeyed, my head spinning—why is it always the prevalent sensation around this man?

Another picture flew across the room and landed on the table. I looked at it and saw it was one of Robert.

Roland took another chair and pulled it up to the table, informing me that Quiggley was in my house and spreading his anger over it. I asked why he was angry and was told that was exactly what we were going to attempt to discover.

Roland stretched his arms across the table and grasped my hands in his. They were warm to the touch. Between them lay the picture of Robert, gazing up at me with innocent eyes. I silently asked him to please protect our home as another object came sailing across the table, nearly hitting me; whatever it was it crashed onto the floor just outside the parlor with resounding impact. Roland warned me to be wary of flying debris, and I almost laughed at the ridiculousness of his statement. Yes, I was very set on keeping my head down.

"Quiggley!" he called out, his voice firm and loud, like a military officer issuing a command on a battlefield. "This woman's house is not for you to destroy! Stop this childish display and tell us what you want!"

Incredibly, the flying objects stopped and the air seemed to grow calm again. I looked around and watched with growing dread as the light seeped out of the room and darkness took its place. I asked how that could be—it was around noontime. Roland replied that it took a powerful presence to do that.

He called out again to the old man, asking him what he wanted, why he had followed me home. The air in the house seemed to swirl about, disturbed and angry. Things moved all around us, objects lifted up from where they sat and then thumped back down again. Thankfully, none of them sailed across the room. My sense of it was that he—Quiggley—was *thinking*. He was perhaps mulling the questions over. I prayed that he reached a favorable verdict, and my home would be spared any more of his tantrum.

The picture of Robert shifted on the table, and spun around to face Roland. He nodded, as if he understood something.

"Yes, I see it," he said. "But why this man? Why Robert Randolph? Was he your friend in life? Possibly your only friend?"

I thought back to things my husband had told me about Quiggley, about talks they'd had, and how the old man was different with him than any of the other men at the Ironworks. Quiggley had favored Robert to some extent. I said this out loud to Roland, and when I did the picture rotated again, this time to face me. My companion whispered to me that I seemed to have the spirit's attention.

"I wish I knew what you wanted, sir," I said to the air around us. "My husband was very fond of you. I would like to help you if I can. Robert would have liked that."

Almost instantly, a great sob sounded throughout the parlor. If I

107

hadn't heard it with my own ears, I would never have believed it. It was just as if a living human being had expressed great anguish right there in the room, as loud as can be. I felt immediately saddened, so filled with pain was it. Roland responded by squeezing my hands, quietly urging me to continue. But continue with what? What in the world was I actually doing?

Calming myself and trying to organize my thoughts, I asked very delicately who the woman and child in his tintype were—were they the reason for his sadness and anger?

Roland stared at me intently all the while, his face a stony mask; I could almost see his brain working behind it, somehow sending me support through the darkness. He whispered for me to be careful with every word I spoke from that moment on.

Another sob came to us, though not as audible as the first one. I felt it more in my body than in my ears. Roland squeezed my hands again, but I wasn't certain what he was telling me with that. Quiggley offered no answers to my question, but at least he wasn't throwing anything more.

Just then I felt Robert in the room.

Tears welled up in my eyes. There was no mistaking it; I always could feel his presence in a room even before I actually saw him. It was more than just his scent. It was something else entirely. Now it was flooding into the parlor and I knew I would be all right. He was shielding me, protecting me. As he always did.

"Thank you, Robert,' said Roland, looking up from the table and past me. I wondered if he could see him over my shoulder, but resisted the urge to turn and look—I knew the story of Orpheus very well from my childhood. I waited, hoping that if spirits did indeed walk the Earth, they could come to the aid of their loved ones. In my mind, I thanked him, too, and asked him to take his friend Quiggley in hand and help him to see the light, if that was possible. Perhaps, I thought, the man could see the woman and child again, if they had passed beyond.

Roland spoke up, his words so odd, yet also necessary for some reason: "Go to thy rest, oh shade. Thou have served well in life; now take thy reward."

Light came back into the room when he had finished, and the feeling of a very great weight being lifted from my home. I found myself crying and asking Roland if Robert had to go, also. He squeezed my hands once more, and gave me a sad smile. "Only if he wants to, Marie. Only if he wants to."

Later, after everything looked normal again, I moved about the house while restoring it the best I could, thinking on how everything had changed in only a few minutes. To Roland I noted our failure to discover the secret of the woman and child's identities, and he agreed it was unfortunate but unavoidable given the circumstances. I also told him the words he spoke there at the end were so very pretty—where did he learn them?

The man just looked at me, shook his head, and with complete honesty in his eyes said he truly didn't know. He had never heard or said them before today.

Summer

THE OLD TRACK

June 24

The first day of summer in Jordan came and went without much
fanfare, save for a series of thunderstorms that drove us indoors and
away from the park and picnics and other pastimes. I found the
weather suited my mood, as it was still somewhat darkened by the
events of that day more than a month ago. No, I just wasn't feeling
myself—"out of sorts" is how Robert would have put it.

My writing has come and gone, too. I'm not certain why I ever
started it in the first place, but it's always seemed like a natural thing
to do and while the muse often eludes me when I do write I feel
engaged. That is, when I'm not in a mood, and this particular mood
provided no inspiration for writing.

I can only describe it as a feeling of detachment, that I'd somehow lost my sense of self after the day I helped drive a spirit out of
my home...or at least that's what I believe I did. Only one other
person can say for sure, and until today it had been several weeks
since I'd not seen hide nor hair of Mr. Roland James. As far as I
knew, he'd left Jordan following that terrible day, or perhaps he'd
just gone to ground and avoided all human contact. I wouldn't have
been surprised either way.

As summer approached, I searched for things to occupy my time,
and in doing so I rediscovered the town of Jordan. It had been my
home for several years, but while I crisscrossed it day after day looking into its market, its shops, its bakery, library, and more, I felt as
if I was seeing it for the first time. And of course, I saw the indelible
stamp of Jordan on every bit of it. It is the company's town, through
and through, a thought that led me to another: Virginia Jordan.

I missed the girl. I hadn't known her long, but I felt she was a
kindred spirit of a type, and maybe she thought the same of me. She
was an only child and often seemed very lonely, but when her mind
was captured by something she clasped it to herself and hung on.
I remember talking about books with her and her description of a
poet she had so fallen in love with she hunted down each and every
one of his books. Well, if truth be told, Virginia had her father do

the hunting as he traveled back and forth across the country on company business. I'm sure that contributed greatly to her loneliness.

Russell Jordan. I began to think a lot about him to over the dying days of spring, and why no one had seen him since Virginia's abduction. It also struck me, just today in fact, that I'd heard little of the girl's *adventures* in the past year or so, which struck me as odd considering they were the talk of the town year in and year out. Of course, my mind had been occupied by other things over the past year, but still…I then made up that mind to find out what our Miss Jordan had been up to in the wider world.

Stepping into the Jordan News office, I was surprised to see Mr. Roland James standing there, as comfortable in his skin as any man I'd ever seen. He greeted me with a bow of his head from his neck and addressed me as "Mrs. Randolph." I was glad for that; my mood didn't allow for first names. As I offered my own polite greeting, our editor-in-chief stepped into the room and Mr. James turned to acknowledge him. As he did, I saw a Negro standing just behind him, apparently accompanying him.

The man tipped his hat to me, but wouldn't meet my eyes, just offering me a "Ma'am." All at once I realized I'd seen him on two separate previous occasions: once in the train station on the first day of spring, and then at the Ironworks the day my ghost-hunter and I visited. Why I should recognize him I cannot say, but I cared less for talking to him than I did Mr. James. I also could not understand why the two would be together. Regardless, he apologized for not calling on me, and I assured him it wasn't necessary that he do so. This caused him to look at me strangely, but I ignored him and, bidding him a good day, turned around to leave. The newsman asked me if there was something I wanted from him, but I told him it wasn't important and could wait.

Just as I was exiting, Mr. James asked if I had sensed Robert was still with me. I should have walked right out there and then and not given him the satisfaction of a response, any response, but instead I wheeled around and told him in no uncertain terms I didn't wish to speak of my husband around strangers, and gave the Negro a quick, pointed look. Mr. James, thinking I was asking for an introduction, began to offer one, but at that moment I chose to leave the office.

I walked away wondering why he was still in Jordan and what he was doing at the newspaper. I also cursed my luck—I really did want to catch up on any news of Virginia and didn't exactly relish the idea of asking my neighbor Mrs. Soames if she knew anything.

Roland James appeared at my elbow less than a minute after I stormed away from him. I barely glanced at him, primarily to see if the Negro was with him. The man was not present, but I kept on walking. My anger had cooled somewhat, but I'd made up my mind to not give my old friend the time of day. He asked my forgiveness if he'd been rude. I assured him he had not, but that I'd had my fill of ghosts and spirits and wanted a normal life from now on, thank you very much. And to please never bring Robert up again.

"I'm looking into the matter of Quiggley's tintype, Marie," he said quietly. "And yes, keeping a low profile. A company town is a very insular thing, and Jordan isn't quite as outgoing as it may seem on the surface."

I stopped and turned to face him, looking at his face, his one eye, his patch, and his hatless head of hair. It needed cutting. I thanked him for his apology, and wished him the very best of fortune in his inquiries. Perhaps we'd see each other again someday.

Then, without giving him the opportunity to say anything more, I headed home once again, planning dinner and tomorrow's excursions and an afghan I planned to crochet, anything but involving myself in the man's latest compulsion to do whatever it is exactly he does.

July 3

Thankfully, I have also been kept busy over the last several weeks by being involved with the planning for our town's summer picnic. Today that investment of time paid off when a splendid time was had by all—except, perhaps, Roland James.

Jordan is like many other towns that hold a little summer celebration for its citizens in that we have a time for eating, for games and singing, for fireworks, and even for just relaxing and enjoying the day. Robert was always very much involved in all aspects of the picnic, and because of that I became a part of it, too. This year I found myself looking forward to it, to begin to truly integrate myself back into the community and throw off the last vestiges of my mourning. The weather cooperated fantastically and the sun helped lift the darkness from my shoulders. That is until Mr. James made an appearance.

I sighed audibly when I saw him from across the field next to the park, dressed in his usual odd clothes, patch on his eye and no hat. I admit I resisted a smile, reminding myself I was still unhappy with him. He spotted me after a few minutes of mingling along the edges of the celebration and started toward me. I lowered my eyes and swung my attention to the small stage that had been set up near the bandstand.

Up on the stage gathered a crowd of children, a collection of sons and daughters from among Jordan's most well-known townsfolk, but also, as I saw with some surprise, two Negro youths, a boy and a girl. I wondered what they were doing with the others, for I knew the children had planned a little play, something of a historical nature from what I understood.

A shadow fell over me just then, and I looked up to see Mr. James standing there, asking me why I was frowning. I began to tell him I was questioning the mixing of the children, but decided it was none of his business. Instead I simply greeted him politely, but without warmth. He asked if he could sit down at my table. Glancing around to see if anyone nearby might be looking at us, I decided no real harm could come of it and indicated a spot across the table from me. He sat.

We stared at each other for a moment, and finally I told him "I'm not interested in pursuing the matter any further."

The man considered that, smiled, and said he himself had no choice; he was bound to follow any thread he could for an answer to the mystery. I let that pass, unsure of why he would be "bound" by such a thing, but made very certain he understood I did not appreciate any sullying of Robert's good name and reputation. I believed he had previously implied something controversial, to put it mildly, and I would not allow him to continue along that line of thought. My husband was good and true; I knew this as I knew myself.

"Marie," he said, leaning closer, "you could not be more wrong in your opinion of me. I am not suggesting your Robert had anything to do with that woman and child—" Here I insisted he lower his voice. "—but rather that Quiggley looked upon him as something more than just a friend."

His words struck me, and instead of letting myself grow angry, I pondered them. Presently, I suggested that my husband was seen as a kind of son to the old man. Mr. James liked that very much, I could see, and he looked on me with his good eye with favor, as if suddenly he'd seen something he hadn't seen before.

He grew silent and I looked back at the stage to see the Negro children running back and forth with the others. This prompted him to note I was frowning again. I told him to never mind and would he care to get me some punch?

When he returned with two glasses of the fruity drink, he surprised me by saying he'd heard rumor of Mr. Russell Jordan himself making an appearance at the picnic. I in turn informed him I believed there'd be little chance of that, as the man hadn't been seen for the past few years. He grew quiet again, and then: "What of Mrs. Jordan?"

I couldn't see where his line of thinking was headed, especially after changing tracks from Quiggley to the Jordan family, but all I could tell him about Mr. Jordan's wife was that she died only a year or so after giving birth to Virginia, the couple's only child. This apparently satisfied my ghost-hunter, for he didn't continue with further questions in that area, but in lieu of talking turned toward the stage and applauded as the children began their little drama.

When the play was over, we ate a pleasant meal of cold salmon sandwiches, cucumber salad, cheese, and currant tarts. The latter of which I enjoyed very much and complimented Mrs. Soames on the recipe. She thanked me and gave Mr. James an odd look, scanning him from stern to aft.

And no, Russell Jordan did not put in an appearance, though I heard his name bandied about today more so than normal in town. While he is the founder of Jordan, of course, mentions of the man have tapered off considerably recently, so that his name was on the tip of so many tongues was puzzling.

Later, after the fireworks, I turned back to my companion to find he was gone, vanished into thin air like the spirits he hunted. I shrugged and got up from my lawn chair, dusted myself off and went over to my fellow organizers to compliment them on a successful picnic. I also added a note of query as to why the Negroes had made themselves part of the proceedings.

Mrs. Graymalkin, one of the committee members, then said the queerest thing to me: "Why, my dear Mrs. Randolph, why ever would you ask such a thing? It was you yourself who invited them!"

July 6

I awoke this morning with a headache, due mostly to bad dreams throughout the night. After breakfast, I spent nearly twenty minutes looking for the writings I had done last year, but, inexplicably, they were nowhere to be found anywhere in the house. Giving up finally, I hoped it all wouldn't darken my day, and took a headache powder to insure it wouldn't. I had work ahead of me.

My companions for the day were to be the Soames boys once more, as their mother had fallen leaving the summer picnic and strained her ankle. They boys, she told me, were being rambunctious and full of the season, and with them on holiday from school, she just *couldn't* look after them properly...and, *oh*, Marie—could you entertain them?

Of course I could, seeing as how I am currently without any charges and feeling a bit of the season myself. The outside called to me, and perhaps the picnic nudged me back into the land of the living a bit. It could be fun, I told myself, just as long as Uly didn't want to go to the train station for the hundredth time.

"Train station!" both lads shouted in unison when I asked them what they wanted to do today. I looked at them in dismay at first, but when I narrowed my eyes and asked if they were *certain* that's what they were keen to do, both of them—even Michael—nodded their heads emphatically and assured me there was no better place to go in all of Jordan. I wish I knew exactly what it is they see in the place, or what they see in repeated visits to it. Personally, I could have done without it, especially considering my dreams last night: *I dreamt I was on a train.*

The day was quite warm, hot even, and I took a parasol to keep the sun off my face and my headache at bay. They boys behaved themselves admirably on the walk to the station, and I mused my regular musings as we passed the various Jordan landmarks. Once at the station, Uly proclaimed he was to be the tour guide and began to show Michael and myself around the place, as if we had never seen it before. I studied the younger Soames and decided he'd grown out of his timidness concerning the station, which had to be a good thing.

As we passed a large window looking out over the tracks, I noticed two figures walking along one that was the farthest out from the station. I watched as they strode alongside one of the rails, talking animatedly to each other and periodically pointing to a spot off in the distance where the track curved away and disappeared around an outcropping of rock. Looking in the same direction, I couldn't see what they were gesturing at and returned to looking at the two men themselves. I knew them; or at least I knew one and was vaguely acquainted with the other.

Roping in Uly long enough to tell him I was stepping outside for a moment and that his brother was never to be out of his sight, I exited the main station to walk down the long deck between the tracks and toward Mr. James and his Negro companion.

"Fate seems to have thrown us together once more," I called out to our resident spirit-chaser, adding that I hoped he'd gained the permission of the station master to walk the tracks. They frowned on such things, and at the very least it was a poor example to any children who might be looking on. I received a shy smile from the man in response, as if he were a child caught in doing something he wasn't supposed to be. This warmed something in me and I found myself unable to whip up my previous anger at him. He'd behaved himself at the picnic, more or less, and almost seemed, well, normal. Only he could maintain that throughout one entire conversation.

He introduced the Negro as Raymond Jones; I gave him a nod. Mrs. Graymalkin's words at the picnic came back to me and I could feel my cheeks flush a bit. As a way of getting past the awkward introduction, I asked Roland what he was doing walking the tracks on such a nice summer's day. To my amazement, he appeared at a loss for words to explain it. Or, he didn't care to let me in on it.

But why should he? I chided myself for thinking he would tell me anything about his business at all—where did such an assumption come from? Yes, we had shared an "adventure" together, and he'd always appeared willing, even eager, to involve me in the things he was pursuing, but that didn't mean it was to continue indefinitely.

A bit crestfallen, I wished him and Mr. Jones happy hunting and turned to go back into the station to fetch the boys. As I did, Roland called after me.

"Marie, I apologize,' he said, and sounded contrite. "It's just that I'm honestly not sure what I'm looking for."

I told him it was all right, that he didn't owe me a thing, and continued on my way. I was almost to the doors to the station when he called out again.

"It's just that—that I had a *dream* last night. About a track. A train track." He paused searching for the words. "We *both* did, Raymond and I. The exact same dream."

I stood still, my hand on the doorknob. Then, I turned around and walked back to him, asking if he'd tell me more about the dream and what he thought it meant. Roland looked at me, his eye searching mine, like he'd done before, except I didn't remember it feeling so unnerving.

With a faltering tone, which was strange coming from him, he explained that at the present moment he couldn't say just what it meant, but it wasn't pleasant. The dream involved a track that wasn't used, an old track, perhaps abandoned, yet a train rode its rails and he had ridden that train. It went past houses and people, yet no one it passed seemed to notice the train.

"And so that's what I'm—we're doing out here," he said, indicating the Negro. "Raymond, for some reason, had nearly the same, identical dream." Mr. Jones confirmed that and said nothing like that had happened to him before. He liked trains, and had never had a nightmare about them in all his days.

"Well," I told them both, "you won't find anything like that out here." I pointed to the tracks arrayed around the station. "But there's something like that near my house."

You would have thought Roland James had never heard anything so remarkable as he jumped up off the track and ran toward me with the most incredulous look on his face.

July 7

A sense of purpose greeted me this morning, and as I slipped out of my bed I began to arrange the order of things for the day.

First was to enlist the Soames brothers in our search. I was to have the day with them anyway, so I reasoned they might enjoy helping us out back. Second was to meet with Roland at the prearranged time of eleven o'clock. I was pleasantly surprised when he informed me yesterday that waiting until this morning for our search would be fine, and that late morning would be best of all.

And so, shortly before eleven I gathered Uly and Michael from their home, told them what I had planned, and started off on our short trek across my property to the very back of it. It was already very warm, though the sun darted in and out of the clouds hinting that it may just decide to rain.

The property is overall very narrow, but long, mostly flat, and ends just about where a large thatch of woods begin. There are also several hillocks where the trees approach my land, and these gradually form more proper hills as they recede into the distance. It makes for a lovely view out the rear windows of my house.

Roland and his Negro companion arrived just at eleven, walking out of the woods toward us. Seeing them both together I was somewhat glad the back of my property isn't easy to see from the neighbors' windows. Roland seemed a bit pensive; I saw he carried a rolled-up piece of paper and wondered what it could be. Uly stopped and stared at Mr. Jones, but I could tell he was interested in meeting him. Michael didn't know what to make of either man and hung back with me, watching to see how I was reacting before deciding how to approach the matter himself.

"I wonder if this might not be a fool's errand, Mrs. Randolph," Roland announced as he stepped up to me and wiped at his brow. Hardly a proper greeting to start the day, but I forgave him and asked him what he meant. Holding out the rolled paper, he unfurled it and pointed, explaining that he'd spent the remainder of yesterday researching railroad tracks in and around Jordan and there was no evidence on record of any track ever in the vicinity of my home. No, I insisted; I had seen the track I spoke of myself and both Robert and I could not have misidentified it. It was somewhere nearby, at the edge of my property, and we had only to find it.

The search began. I headed for the area I roughly remembered it to be, and the two brothers followed me, laughing and casting their eyes all about. The two men cast themselves off in another direction, yet not far from where the boys and I were looking. We set about it in earnest, but after fifteen minutes or so of grass and sand and dirt and rocks I began to despair a bit. Perhaps I'd been wrong after all, though deep down I didn't feel I was. Glancing over at Roland, I bit my lip and continued the quest, feeling a trifle tad foolish.

Finally, after a good half-hour of searching, Uly whooped and shouted "Here! Here! Look here!"

All five of us convened over the spot and gazed down at a piece of dark metal, long and flat on top, showed itself through the earth. Roland knelt down and ran his fingers over it, pushing some dirt away from it to reveal even more length. He looked up at the Negro and nodded; Mr. Jones nodded back. Then, standing up again, he congratulated me. I in turn asked him to give his praise to Uly for finding it.

A shadow of a cloud passed over us as the boys wandered off to find more "treasure" and I asked Roland if anything about it seemed familiar. He shook his head and started off walking along the length of the track—that is, where that length would be if it were visible beyond the patch we could see. The ground itself showed little sign of the metal piece beyond the spot, meaning no mounded dirt or the like. In fact, as Roland walked off I wondered if its twin was still in existence running alongside of it, yet buried and out of sight.

I shook off my reverie when I heard Roland curse. I looked over to him standing several yards away looking intently at a small hillock that rose up in front of him. Then, he got to his knees and began digging in the dirt. A moment later and Mr. Jones joined him. Behind me, a small voice told me he was bored and could he and Michael do something else? Yes, I said to Uly; go back to the house and find a good book for the two of them to read until I was done.

There was also lemonade in the icebox, I added.

With the little ones out of my hair, I walked over to the men and asked what was the matter. "The track simply...ends," said Roland with a frown. "There seems to be nothing particularly special about it, besides its age and that the world seems to have forgotten it."

I wondered aloud what he'd hoped to find in the first place. Confirmation of some part of his dream? A buried locomotive to go with the rails? I stopped when I saw his face; he looked as if he thought I was mocking him, but I assured him I was only curious and a bit bewildered. As he was about to reply, Mr. Jones' deep voice cut through the moment to ask Roland to come quickly—he'd found something.

We turned to look around at where the man could be, and then Roland trotted around the hillock and called after me to follow. When we rejoined the Negro, he was pointing at the ground, running his index finger back and forth to indicate another partially buried rail...and its twin.

The rails headed toward the woods, which ran right up to the spot we stood upon. I peered into them, and thought they looked a bit dark and foreboding, as well as tightly packed with trees and shrubs and tall grasses. Looking back at the track then, I must admit the deepening mystery of it all was exciting. Roland felt it too, but I think he was containing himself, trying to be cool and calm about it. Rubbing at his chin with a finger and turning his head back and forth from the woods to the hillock we'd just come around, he asked Mr. Jones to please take a position at the top of the mound and, if possible, confirm that the two tracks we'd found appeared to be one and the same line.

I watched the man walk away and begin to ascend the summit. By the time I turned my head back around to say something to Roland about our good fortune, he was gone.

I called out to him, my heart starting to beat faster. Where could he have run off to? I saw no sign of him at all, not even footprints in the dirt. For some reason I gazed down the length of the rails, trying to imagine why they would point toward the woods—could the tall, densely packed trees actually have grown up since the track was abandoned? It didn't seem right...

And then all of a sudden Roland was back. I blinked and there he was, walking away from the woods and down the middle of the rails to my position, a very queer expression on his face.

"Valerie," he said, "I have just seen something truly astounding."

My ears must have deceived me, and so I asked him what to repeat the name he'd just used. He reddened and apologized. "Marie—Marie…how strange."

With that he walked past me, turning his head to address me once again.

"And Marie, could you possibly join me here again tomorrow, on this same spot, say ten o'clock??"

Damn the man.

July 8

Roland James was in the predetermined spot at the proscribed time. While his smile was not quite that of the cat that ate the canary, he had the look of a man who knew something no one else did and was eager to share it. I approached him with some trepidation, but also with a good dose of curiosity.

He bid me a good morning, standing there in his odd suit of clothes under the rising summer sun, and told me Raymond Jones would not be joining us today. Then, asking if I was ready, he noted the mostly hidden steel rail on the ground, the hillock just beyond it, and had me fix both in my mind's eye before we proceeded. When I assured him I was ready and intrigued, he started off walking around the hill toward the woods. Dutifully, I followed.

On the other side, we walked the length of the other section of track we'd found yesterday and arrived at the spot where it ended just before the closely packed treeline. Stepping up to me, he asked my permission to place his hand on my shoulder. I told him to go ahead. His hand was warm and solid as an anchor. Then, turning me in place so that we faced away from the trees and toward the track, he leaned in close to tell me to look at the rails and connect both sections, the one there and the one on the other side of the hillock, in my mind.

"Have you fixed it there, Marie?" he asked. "All right. Now, we will be slowly taking one step backward together, and then a second, and…"

I maintained my focus on the track before us, trying to ignore the idea of stepping somewhere I couldn't see. Branches came into view at the very edges of my vision and then…

…we were *elsewhere*.

I gasped. Where once were the track and the hill and blue skies with nary a cloud, there was a wall of green, a musky smell of earth, and shifting shadows that darted to and fro across my vision. I blinked and the world utterly changed in that instant.

My knees buckled and I must have said something. Roland was reaching out to grab me by the arms and support me, assuring me in a calm, steady voice that I was fine, *we* were fine, and to try not to be frightened.

Head swimming, I stuttered out questions as he held me up: Where? How? *Can we get back?*

"Most assuredly, Marie,' he replied with conviction. "I found my way back yesterday and have no doubt I can do it again. I would not have brought you here if I'd any reason to believe you would be in any danger." He paused, staring at me intently. "Are you ready to take a look around?"

With his help, I began to turn myself. To my right was a sloping wall of earth that rose up and away from us, green but uneven, definitely not for climbing easily. As I continued to turn I caught sight of a length of railroad track on the ground that stretched away from the spot upon which we stood and off into the distance. Mostly uncovered, the steel rails looked old and worn, but still sturdy. Now fully turned around from our entry point, I gazed down the track and saw that the slope of earth, now on my left, ran alongside the rails as far as I could see and at its uppermost part where it leveled out again stood a dense growth of thick trees. In all the slope was more than ten feet tall and the trees along it grew so high I had to crane my neck to look up to their tops. To the right of the track was another line of similar trees, but growing up from the same level as the rails and meeting the opposite trees to form a dark, green canopy of sorts that reminded me of the ceiling of a great cathedral, majestic and solemn.

Light broke through the uppermost branches of the trees here and there, creating the shifting patchwork quilt of shifting shadows that spread out over the queer place, fueled by a wind that blew from somewhere beyond the treetops. I could hear it, very slightly, but no other sounds; there was no birdsong or chatter of small animals at all, just the creaking of branches far above our heads and that far-off whisper of the wind.

In all it made for a gloomy tableau. I shuddered and looked at Roland with eyes that surely showed my concern. He nodded and attempted to explain what had happened.

"Yesterday," he said, still holding me by the arms with both hands, "I was standing where we stood before we came here and attempting to connect the two lengths of old track in my mind. That must have been a catalyst of a kind, for when I absentmindedly took a step or two backward at that point, I wound up *here*."

Not really comprehending anything he was telling me—how could I?—I asked him how he got back. "Well, I *willed* myself back, Marie," he said with a small note of disbelief that did little to assure me I could do the same. "Don't worry; I am with you and I won't let any harm come to you."

"But where *are* we?" I implored him.

"I really don't know," he replied.

I stared out at the scene before us, shaking my head and shuddering again at the thought of what it all meant and the thought that such a place could exist where such a place should *not*. Seeking some refuge, some port in the storm, I grasped his hand in mine and tried to hold onto my sanity.

"Now then," Roland said with an earnest look that was meant to cheer me, "are you ready to take a little walk?"

Too stunned to argue, I motioned for him to begin, and slipped my arm in his to insure my ability to stay upright. In that fashion we ambled on our way, two people walking into Wonderland. For the first few feet I kept my eyes on the ground and the tracks there, too afraid to look up, but when Roland prompted me, assuring everything was all right, I raised my head to look forward—and immediately saw figures far up ahead of us.

Roland must have felt me tense myself and asked what was wrong. I pointed at the figures; they appeared to be people, but because of the distance and the odd, dappled lighting of the place I couldn't see them clearly. I blinked, trying to clear my eyes, but they were gone as if they were never there.

My companion nodded and held fast to me. "Our eyes may play tricks on us here," he told me. "We must be careful of what we see… and what we believe we see."

I lifted my free hand and pointed up ahead again, asking him if what

I was seeing just then was something we should believe or disbelieve.

We both watched as a light sifted through the trees some several yards forward from where we were. The light was more like a glow, actually, poking its way around the trees next to the track, growing and receding, pulsing as if alive. Roland began to walk faster and I made an effort to keep pace with him lest he leave me behind, and in *that* place I wanted nothing less than to not be alone.

Presently we arrived on the spot of the diffusion of light and looked straight at it as we stood in the middle of the two rails. The tree trunks there seemed to *waver* in the air, not unlike what one might see when looking at something through intense heat, although the temperature was the same throughout the entire place, apparently. Roland stretched out his arm to cross it over in front of me, a gesture of protection that I appreciated, not knowing what the effect we were viewing meant. Then, before my eyes, the tree trunks melted away and I saw a house beyond them, perhaps only a few yards away.

Roland sucked in his breath, clearly affected by the phenomenon. I was so stunned I lost my voice again and simply stood there mute as the house became clearer to us, though not familiar, I realized. Forcing myself to speak, I asked Roland if it was real, if it was really and truly there, or something unreal and therefore not to be believed. He could offer no assurance as to its reality, only noted that it might be a kind of ghost, or an image from the past caught in the web of the weird place.

Apparently, we were there to witness some occurrence, for then the wall of the house that faced us melted away not unlike the trees and we were treated to a view inside the dwelling, and the two people therein.

The man and woman—I did not recognize them, either, though I could see the man worked at the Ironworks—were arguing. The man sat at a kitchen table, bending over a glass with an amber-colored beverage, clearly inebriated. The woman stood a few feet away; I got a sense of her keeping her distance. She was saying the man—her husband, no doubt—should have asked for more money from his employer. He in turn defended himself, and rather loudly.

It went back and forth, their words volleying to and fro, but none of them scoring. I could feel my face flush from the embarrassment of our eavesdropping on the private conversation, and my impression was that Roland felt the same.

But we continued to watch and listen, mesmerized by the scene. It continued for some minutes until the man swept the glass off the table and sent it crashing to the floor. Getting up from his chair he pushed past the woman, nearly knocking her over, and exited through a door which he slammed behind him. The woman, in tears, collapsed in a heap on the floor, and whispered something.

I swear the words were "Curse Russell Jordan. He doesn't care a thing for us."

I must have been concentrating so intently on making out the words that I didn't see her next action until I felt Roland buck in alarm. Looking up, I saw the woman reach up to the nearby countertop and slide an object off it and into her hand.

It was a knife. A very sharp-looking knife which she placed at her throat and held it there while the angry tears flowed down her cheeks.

"Oh, *Roland!*" I shouted, but as I did the light of the tableau went dim and the woman, the knife, the room, and the house all faded from view to be replaced once more by the quiet, tranquil, unmoving trees.

I shook all over in a quiver of desperate tension—was it happening *now*, somewhere in Jordan? And where was Jordan? We needed to go back and…and…

All I remember then is Roland telling me it was time to leave the place. I could only agree and no more. I was numb and could not muster any more care or concern about anything at all.

July 12

Roland and I walked back to my house on that unprecedented day, both deep in our own thoughts. My very great relief at being able to exit that place, which I have come to think of as the Old Track, was overshadowed by my anguish over what I had seen. With every step I took back into the real world I dreaded the news of a suicide in town and prayed the woman, whoever she is, stopped before going too far with her own great sorrow and sparing her precious life.

To this moment, four days later, there has been no news of such an event. Jordan is a small place after all, and if one of our neighbors had taken such a drastic step, we would all know of it within hours.

Who is she? Surely she and her husband live in Jordan, for they talked about our founder and furthermore, seemed to refer to him in the present, meaning of course his absence from public activity. I sympathized with the couple: Robert and I had more contact with the man than others, but his shunning of his own town is still hurtful.

But perhaps the woman isn't real in the first place. Perhaps I shall never know.

That night I fell asleep almost immediately, and soon entered a dream that seemed to go on forever. It was a train again, but not like on the Old Track; it was an actual train, and I was on it with Roland—though he had two good eyes—and Raymond Jones. The Negro was dressed in a uniform of some kind, strangely, and when I awoke the next morning I found myself wishing to see him. This thought troubled me immensely, for on one hand it felt so very wrong, yet on the other I felt a connection with him and needed to find out why such a bond would exist at all.

When Roland left me at my home, he indicated his intention to return to the Old Track, but only after a day or so of rest and reflection. A surge of anxiety welled up in me at his words and I wrung a promise from him that he would not return there without me. He agreed, albeit reluctantly, but I could tell deep down he knew that I was part of it, that whatever it was that existed out there at the edge of my property, we were both entangled in it…and, somehow, so too was Raymond Jones.

Three days later, yesterday, I received a note from a message boy saying that Roland would meet me at the spot today, this morning.

The two men waited for me there, Roland with his characteristic slight smile and the Negro stony faced. I greeted them both and told them of my dream. Mr. Jones nodded as if he understood, but our ghost-hunter furrowed his brow and pursed his lips as if to say something. Ultimately he did not. I asked if we should get under way, and Jones crooked both his arms, obviously intending Roland and myself to each take one. Without hesitation I stepped to Roland's side and took his arm, while he reached out and took the Negro's arm. As a linked trio we positioned ourselves with our backs to the woods and our eyes on the track.

Just as the time before, the scene changed and I knew without a doubt we were back in the strange glade of the Old Track.

We all three released each other's arms and turned in place to face the track. Everything was exactly as it was when I last visited—the track, the tall slope on its left, and the trees on the same level of it to its right. The shifting shadows from the branches above reminded me of a moving stained glass window.

Without further ado we began to walk, and to my slight surprise Roland offered his hand to me, and I slipped my own into it. It made me feel secure, but also a touch salacious. Pushing aside the thought I straightened my spine and looked ahead down the long track. As I expected, I caught a fleeting glimpse of the same sort of moving figures as the last time, but they were gone when I tried to focus on them.

"I saw them, too," said Mr. Jones, unbidden. I presume Roland had informed him of the phenomenon before we entered the area.

We walked. At one point I believed we passed the spot where we'd stood and witnessed the man and woman in the house, but I couldn't be sure and we didn't pause there. If Roland recognized it, too, he gave no indication. Instead, he appeared to be wholly focused on the track ahead of us and so I didn't disturb him. We continued to walk and after a while I presumed we'd been traveling for an hour or more, which I said aloud to my companions.

Roland considered this. "And I feel no fatigue," he said, and then took out a pocket watch and glanced at it. "And my watch has stopped. Raymond?"

The Negro confirmed his had also, and just to make it consistent I checked my own small watch and saw it too had stopped at the moment we entered the glade. Raymond spoke up again to point our attention at the track; many feet ahead of us it began to curve to the right.

As we entered the curve I heard what I believed to be music, which startled me for we hadn't heard any such thing before. The men must have heard it too, because we moved in unison at a faster pace and saw a light up ahead of us, just as we did the other day. Roland advised me to approach the scene with caution and to be ready for any eventuality. I digested that, and attempting to temper my steps, I looked forward to seeing what the Old Track had in store for us today.

We stopped in front of the light coming through the tree trunks there and very soon they faded from view to reveal what I thought at first was simply more foliage. Then I discerned a structure behind the trees and shrubs, almost completely hidden by them, and heard Raymond shift in place and say, "I know this place, Roland."

That greenery eventually spirited itself away and the music suffused the air all around us, strange and ghostly itself. It was a kind of spritely thing, a tune on some stringed instrument that wove in and out of our ears and danced over and above us. Just as I tried to place the instrument I saw the house it emanated from, a shanty of ill use and repair, sitting somewhat lopsided on uneven ground. With a flash of insight, and with the help of Jones' statement, I knew it to be a structure in Jordan's Negro district.

The outer wall melted away and a tableau revealed itself: several dark-skinned people sitting around a wooden coffin sitting on top of two crudely made yet sturdy looking stands. Off to one side, at the head of the pine box, a young Negro girl with close-cropped hair and dressed in a simple shift with a blue flower pattern played the instrument we'd been hearing. It was a wooden piece shaped like an hourglass with sound holes and silvery frets, a compact thing that sat across the girls upper legs while she strummed its strings with one hand and the long, graceful fingers of her other hand danced across its flat neck. As I watched her fingers and listened to the music, my body wanted to sway to the tune, so mesmerizing was it. I didn't recognize the tune or the instrument itself—I assumed both were as old as the hills and mountains themselves.

The music came to an end, and as the last note died away, the people all got up and after glancing at the coffin—it's lid was covering it—they left the room one by one with nary a look back. This left the girl and her instrument all alone with the box.

After a minute of sitting and staring down at the floor, she got up, set her instrument on her stool, and stepped over to the coffin. I hadn't noticed it before, but there was what looked like a plate of food sitting on the closed lid. The girl stared at the food and then all in a rush she started eating it, one item after another in quick succession until the plate was clean. I heard Roland make a sound, something like an acknowledgement of the act, but I kept my eyes on the girl. She stood there without moving for a moment, and then started to laugh.

The sound shocked me at first, so out of place in the death room of that house. She continued to laugh until it became almost maniacal and unnatural, and it finally devolved into a choking sound and then light coughing. After another minute passed the girl grew silent, but after looking at the door in the room she dug her fingers down under the edge of the coffin's lid and suddenly threw it up and off in an explosive gesture. Raymond Jones started and slapped his hand over his mouth, his eyes wide with what I assumed was surprise...or fright.

The girl stared down into the pine box, though we could not see the person inside. I thought she might start to laugh again, but she only smiled, a big, broad grin that held no sunshine, no warmth or goodwill, only mischief and malevolence. Then, she left the coffin, returned to her stool and instrument, and sat down to play again.

The scene faded away before our eyes as the curtain of trees came back across it, though the music took some time to disappear as we turned and walked away, back to our starting point on Roland's suggestion.

Mr. Jones was quiet as we trod the track, giving us no indication of whether he knew the girl, the other people in the shanty, or whoever was in the pine box.

July 27

Two weeks have passed, in which I came very close to going mad. We left the Old Track that day with a cloud hanging over the three of us, compounded by Roland's chilling words as to what we witnessed. He told us the girl had eaten the deceased's sin in the form of the food on the plate, but he was certain she was not the intended sin-eater, nor did her actions compare to other cases of the ritual he had known. Furthermore, the girl's disturbing behavior cemented something in his mind, that the town of Jordan was ill and getting worse. He feared for it. Those were his exact words: he feared for it and no good could come of it.

We parted just short of my house and I went inside, but avoided sleep. I didn't want to dream of trains and tracks again. I couldn't bear it, not after that time in the glade of the Old Track.

This begs the question, of course, of why I continually seek returning to it.

I stayed awake for nearly two days, and grew frustrated over Roland's lack of a plan to go back to the place. Finally, because I simply could not continue without sleep—Robert would have been disgusted with me, I reckoned—I crawled into my bed and slipped away quickly and effortlessly. And dreamed of trains.

In the middle of that night I awoke to the cold darkness of my bedroom, and quite honestly did not know who I was or where I was. It took me several minutes to piece it together like a jigsaw puzzle, and when I had my answers I also had something else; a burning desire to return to the glade. The problem with that, I realized, was that I had no way of contacting Roland James. None at all. It was absurd and I could have laughed if my feelings of emptiness were not so pronounced that night.

That singular anxiety continued into the morning of the next day, and the day after that, and the day after that, day upon day until this morning, two weeks after I'd seen him last, the man himself appeared at my door and, raising his voice to be heard above the thunder that accompanied a right good storm that was whipping through Jordan, he invited me to go with him down the Old Track.

He offered no explanation for his long absence, and I did not ask for one. The only thing that mattered to me was to be out of my home and off across the yard to the woods. If I looked and acted anxious to him, he was polite enough to say nothing of it. What he did say was that Raymond Jones was not joining us, that he was still too disturbed by what we'd encountered the last time, and that he'd barely gotten any sleep due to nightmares. That time I did laugh, and while there was no mirth behind it, I hoped my companion would not think me cruel.

We went right into the glade without preamble and began a new trek down its rails. As usual, everything there was as it always is, except darker somehow. Perhaps the storm "outside" was affecting it.

There was also a sense of urgency permeating the place, but I admit it might have been me.

A light from between the tree trunks did not present itself immediately, or even shortly, and instead we walked what could have been several miles before the event happened. When it did, we both quickened our pace and arranged ourselves for the viewing. Something electric ran through me, and inwardly I told myself to be calm and composed—very little good feeling had yet to come from the scenes we'd witnessed before.

As the trees ghosted away to show us yet another structure, I recognized it immediately as the caretaker's cottage at the base of the hill on which Russell Jordan's house sat. When we could see inside, it was just as I remembered it, as was the man who sat a desk inside it, George Honeywell. He was older, certainly, but looked as I knew him, though it had been, I believe, a year or more since the last time we saw each other, which could have been at Robert's funeral.

George was drunk, poor soul, and talking to himself as is his habit. I listened intently.

He was saying something about why did he have to "think about *that* today?" and then why did he "do it in the first place?" I didn't know what he was talking about. Then, "He put the pressure on me, damn him," and "best man we had, for all we knew."

135

It was all terribly disjointed, I thought, but a picture finally formed of George having done something he regretted because someone from his past had forced him to do it. I knew next to nothing of the man's background, regrettably, so it made precious little sense to me, other than it may explain a certain sadness which I always believed he wore.

He got up from the table abruptly, his eyes wide and shining, his ear cocked to listen to something in the distance… "What's that? What's that?" he cried. "*Someone is opening the gate!*"

George scrambled for the door, knocking over his chair in the process. Trying to avoid entangling his legs in it, he reached for a coat on a peg by the door and muttered "I'll have their reason an' *that's* for certain…"

Then he had the door open and wind and rain and thunder filled the doorway immediately. Dread came over me—it was storming for him, too. George got himself into the doorway and looked out, presumably at the gate, shouting "What? What? Who is it?" I tried to look myself, but our vantage point was all wrong to allow it, and so I had to trust George as our eyes.

The scene ended with the poor man screaming "No! It *can't* be! Oh, my Lord—oh my Lord…"

Roland pulled me away from the spot telling me I'd been standing there as if rooted and for several minutes. I asked him to take me out, and we walked back down the track to the egress point. When we were back in the outer world, the storm had lessened, but the rain still came down, warm yet unpleasant. Pulling the hood of my coat up over my head, we struck out for the house.

We were almost to the back door when someone called my name and I looked up to see Mrs. Soames running across the wet grass toward us, her eyes wild and her mouth moving. When she got closer, I asked her what was the matter, but she at first could say nothing, just stare at me with the oddest expression on her face. I asked again what was the matter.

"Marie," she cried, "it's incredible! I can hardly believe it. My husband was just called up to the House on the Hill…"

The feeling of dread came over me again, overwhelming and sickening. I nodded and asked her to tell me the rest.

She gulped and took me by the shoulders with both her hands. "She's back, Marie!" she shouted. "*Virginia Jordan has come back!*"

Autumn

THE JORDAN GIRL

September 23

Autumn arrived yesterday. August and much of September slipped by without my notice, and looking back I see the last time I wrote anything here was late July. I also have still not found any of my writings before the first day of spring this year. Perhaps I only dreamed I had ever written anything before then. Almost this entire year has seemed like a dream.

There has been very little work for me since the children went back to school, but I have found odd jobs here and there and been able to put enough aside to get me through the winter. For the past few days, in fact, I have enjoyed a life of leisure; that is to say I have done little save for some reading and knitting and tidying up around the house. Not much to talk about, overall.

I suppose the really big news in Jordan these last several weeks would be the trial.

News of Virginia Jordan's return to her home got out fairly quickly. But honestly, how could it not have? Despite Russell Jordan's money and influence, he wasn't able to contain such news for long, and in short order the wolves circled the camp and the bonfire grew higher and higher.

And yes, Mr. Jordan himself did reappear in public. There was certainly no way for him not to, not with one of the most notorious figures in this country in the last few years once more living under his roof. Attention was inevitable, as was a trial.

I don't pretend to understand all the legalities of it, but the authorities pounced on the news of Virginia's return and there was an immediate outcry for her to stand trial for her activities—those being her accompaniment of Clement Lee Chase, who some call a "Robin Hood for our times," but others one of the worst, most heinous criminals of the past one-hundred years. Regardless, the Jordan girl was to stand trial for, as I understood it, her part in his many and varied crimes of the past few years.

Arguments from both sides, lawyers and officials, grew heated almost immediately and went for nearly two weeks...*should* she be tried, *where* would she be tried, *how* would she be tried, and so on. I kept abreast of the news and wondered if Mr. Jordan was exerting himself through his money and power to influence the circus it was becoming, and then finally it was determined: Virginia Jordan would stand trial, and here in Jordan. It sounded absurd, and made me suspect Jordan money was behind it.

As I said, I admit I didn't understand all the particulars of it.

The selection of the jury lasted at least another two weeks. As it happened, it was difficult for them to find anyone who wasn't sympathetic of Virginia and her ordeal, seeing as how she'd become as much a "folk hero" as her abductor himself. Eventually they managed to seat a jury that both sides agreed upon and the "Trial of the Century" got under way.

In all, despite all the legal wrangling to make it happen, the trial itself was relatively short. Having little else to do and with a personal interest in it, I tried to attend the proceedings every day it was held, though nearly everyone else in town had the same idea. We all squeezed into our little courthouse, somehow, and watched as the circus came to town.

It was at her trial I saw Virginia for the first time since before she'd been taken. I almost didn't recognize her. She was older, of course, a young lady now, but it was more than that. The lawyers had her appear in simple, almost crude apparel, most likely to foster sympathy for her among the jurors, but I saw something in her face that had changed her much more than age and dress; the girl had lived through events the majority of us could never imagine. She was never called as a witness the entire time, and for the most part she sat there and watched the lawyers stand up and down and stared at them dully. Her father looked anxious more times than not, sweating and fanning himself continuously, watching everything with hawk's eyes, ready to pounce if anything dare not go in Virginia's— or rather his—favor.

But it did. The jurors announced they were deadlocked after a day's deliberation and the judge banged his gavel and sent the circus packing. And that was that. Oh, there was an outcry from some and oaths to the effect of a new trial, but the girl was spirited away by her father and much like his own self-exile, we have seen neither hide nor hair of Virginia recently.

For myself, there was one day in the middle of the trial that was designated a break for the important players in it and I took advantage of the time to take the Soames boys on another outing, that time to the Jordan dam. The day was splendid and both young men enjoyed it, and I felt closer to Robert being there. He'd put his heart and soul into the project, and I imagined his handprints up and down the stone blocks.

I also went to the woods at the back of my property and stood in the spot at the end of the tracks and closed my eyes and imagined them whole. I took a step backward and immediately found myself in the brush and the bramble there, a perfectly good dress ruined.

I have not attempted it since.

October 1

I had visitors today, quite unexpectedly.

Imagine my surprise when after a knock at my door I opened it to find Virginia Jordan and her father standing on my porch. I could only stare at the girl, so taken aback to see her, prompting Mr. Jordan to clear his throat and ask if they might come in. I apologized and invited them in, noticing the man's furtive glances all around him as he crossed my threshold.

Virginia embraced me and I stood back to look at her. Up close she was very pale and I could see even more of her burden on her than at the trial. She wore an immaculate green dress that complimented her green eyes and chestnut brown hair, but I received the impression it was uncomfortable for her. Russell Jordan looked much the same as I remembered him, of medium height and balding, though he was a bit more stooped now, and of even less hair. He wore a fixed smile, and his eyes never stopped looking around.

Virginia stepped over to a photo of Robert and picked it up, telling me how sorry she was for my loss, and that she wasn't here at the time of his death. Jordan cleared his throat nervously and asked if there was anything I needed and I assured him I was fine. Then, throwing some caution to the wind, I told Virginia I had so many questions, so many things to ask her.

"I won't talk about *him,*" she snapped, and looked immediately sorry for it. At that very moment it occurred to me how very odd it was that she and her father would appear at my home, given our brief relationship. Still, it was so very good to see her, and I told her so.

"May I be alone with Maria, sir?" she asked her father. I recalled then that she often called me "Maria" when we were together—it was her mother's name, I believe. Mr. Jordan frowned, but said he'd just step out for a smoke. As he exited, I saw him take not only a cigar from inside his coat, but also several folded papers which he was already reading even before the door shut behind him.

Seeing again how uncomfortable Virginia seemed, I invited her into the parlor and we sat down across from each other, or knees almost touching. It amused me to see the girl immediately slip off her high-heeled shoes and scratch at her one foot through her stocking with the other. Then she reached out and took my hands in hers, squeezing them. I almost jumped at how cold they were, and hoped she didn't notice my surprise.

"You were always so kind to me," she said looking down into her lap. "I never forgot that, Maria, and—and I thought of you from time to time while I…"

I assured her she needn't feel shy around me, and she needn't go into any details of her ordeal, only that I could see the strain on her and hoped she could concentrate on simply being home again and the people who loved her.

This prompted Virginia to sigh heavily and lean over to embrace me again. I felt—what did I feel? It's difficult to put into words. Sympathetic? Yes, definitely. Mystified? Yes, that, too, for I couldn't throw off the sensation of the entire situation being wrong somehow. The girl must have felt it, also, because she sat back in her chair, took hold of me with her green eyes and told me what was on her mind.

"Something is hanging over me, Maria. Something I fear will be the death of me."

My inclination was to say most assuredly something—someone—was hanging over her, and his name was Clement Chase. How else could she feel? The criminal was still at large, still running around who-knows-where doing who-knows-what…and quite possibly very unhappy that Virginia had gotten away from him. I wrestled with the thought, watching as from under the collar of her dress she removed a small pendant or locket that hung from a chain and held it in her hand, running her fingers back and forth over it. I didn't remember her having any nervous habits like it before, but again, years had passed—and horrible ones, at that.

I asked if perhaps the Reverend Soames could talk with her about it, but she scoffed at the suggestion and expressed her disdain for the man. Why then tell me? I wondered aloud.

"I'm told you might know someone who could help me," she said very somberly.

Ah, so there it was. I could only guess it was Mrs. Soames, through her husband, who had put the idea in the girl's head. I thought maybe I'd been able to put our resident ghost-hunter behind me, and his entire, strange world, but here he was again, my personal albatross.

After a moment's reflection, I told Virginia I could try to contact the man she meant, but that I couldn't promise he'd come. She brightened a bit at that and thanked me as she stood up. She slipped back into her shoes, stowed the locket away in her dress again, and walked to the front door. Once there, she turned and embraced me again, asking that I send word to her immediately when I knew more. The House on the Hill would always be open to me, she promised.

I looked on as father and daughter walked away from my home, her hand very lightly on his arm, almost as if they were strangers to each other. In a way, after being separated for years by the most incredible circumstances, I suppose they are.

Returning to whatever it was I was doing before that fateful knock on my door, I wondered how in the wide world I was going to bring Roland James into the situation…and if I should.

October 3

In the end, I needn't have gone looking for the man, for he came looking for me. I wasted a good day and a half walking around Jordan, asking around if anyone knew where he might be, and feeling fairly foolish about it. That feeling intensified when just last evening he suddenly appeared at our little postal office in town and acted as if it hadn't been, well, months since I last saw him.

Setting aside my annoyance and my questions, I told him of Virginia Jordan's request, and Roland grew very serious as he contemplated it. I cautioned him about her father, that I knew he wouldn't brook with any charlatanism, and that it was useless for Roland to get his dander up when he knew damn well I wasn't calling him a charlatan—only that Russell Jordan wasn't the sort of man who'd sit still for anything with even a whiff of a put-up job.

Having somewhat shocked my ghost-hunter, he agreed to see the girl and to "keep his theatrics to a bare minimum." I noted that sarcasm ill became him, arranged a time for the meeting, and left to return home. As I had for several weeks, I slept well.

Roland arrived at my home a few minutes early this cool, blustery afternoon and was here when the Jordans arrived. Despite his rather Bohemian appearance, he was all manners and slight charm, and he greeted both father and daughter in a manner that set me at ease. Mr. Jordan was all frowns and paced a bit, but Virginia only had eyes for Roland, something I caught almost immediately. I hoped it wouldn't interfere with anything that would come from the meeting.

"I want to have a séance, Mr. James," the girl said plainly. Her father bellowed her name, his face reddening, but I rushed in to try to soothe him. Roland gave me a surreptitious nod and turned back to Virginia and complimented her locket. It had come out of her dress collar again and into her hand.

I asked everyone to please sit down, hoping that would alleviate some of the tension in the room. When we were all seated, Roland began to talk. Remarkably, it was innocuous things, mostly about the town and how much he liked it and that he was a visitor to it, but made to feel welcome. With that he cast a glance at Mr. Jordan, who frowned even deeper and harrumphed. I could tell the idea of it made him bristle, and Virginia picked up on it, too, asking her father to please be quiet for her sake.

"In fact, sir," said Roland, "could you please leave us for a time? So your daughter and I may talk more freely?"

Russell Jordan looked like he was ready to blow, but when I spoke up again to quell his temper, my companion turned to me to say, "And you, also, Marie—would you mind?"

"I'm not going anywhere," Mr. Jordan announced. "Have you no sense of propriety? My daughter needs a chaperone."

Both Roland and I opened our mouths to protest, but it was Virginia herself who put her foot down and with an even tone that belied her age. She reminded her father that the last few years away had put her far past such conventions. Before I knew it, the man was out the door and gone, perhaps picked up by the wind and carried who-knows-where. As for myself, I lost the battle too, and walked out my back door with the clear sensation of having been evicted from my own home.

The Devil take Roland James, I thought as I walked through my yard, then immediately regretted it. I let my own temper cool as I made my way to the edge of the woods, wondering what he and Virginia were talking about. When I reached the end of my property, I found Raymond Jones looking over the barely hidden train tracks there.

He greeted me with a nod and a "Good afternoon, ma'am," and I returned the greeting, but kept my distance remembering it wasn't my land he stood on and I had no right to ask him what he was do-ing on it. I also reflected on the fact that it had been quite a while since I'd last seen the Negro, and strangely enough…the sight of him was not completely unwelcome. It may have been due to Ro-land's dismissal of me minutes before, but whatever it was I didn't feel like musing upon it.

"I tried to go on the Old Track," Raymond said, clearly sad-dened. "I couldn't for some reason." I told him I had tried, also, and had formed a theory that just one of us attempting the transfer wasn't enough, and that it would take at least two of us, as Roland and I had done. Jones nodded and considered that, looking up and down the length of the track and the hillock. Finally, he looked up at me with his great brown eyes and said, "Would you go with me, then, ma'am?"

And I did, just like that.

As we placed ourselves in the spot for transfer, it struck me that physical contact was normally necessary between Roland and I for success, but before I could say anything about it, Jones read my mind and chivalrously offered his crooked arm, not his hand. I smiled and placed the fingers of my hand lightly on his coatsleeve and aligned the tracks in my mind, assuming he was doing the same. In an instant we were in the glade of the Old Track.

The atmosphere seemed different somehow, but not to any of my regular senses. If my companion felt it, too, he did not note it to me. Glancing at each other, we began to walk.

After a short while of silence between us, I brought up the subject of the scene we all watched together the last time he and I were on the track at the same time, wondering aloud of his reaction to the girl and her sin-eating.

"I wasn't stricken the way you might think, ma'am," he said after a moment of contemplation. "That was my niece. And that was my brother in the box."

I could feel my face flush a bit, and then told him I didn't quite understand—he was affected by his family ties with those people, wasn't he? "No, ma'am," he replied earnestly. "Not because they are my kin, but because they *are* my kin and when I looked upon them I didn't feel *anything*."

His anguish was still interwoven with his words and I imagined how much the idea of family meant to him, and when suddenly he realized he wasn't as moved as he should be over the tribulations we witnessed, well, I began to see what he was saying.

"Light up ahead, ma'am," he said, and I looked up ahead of us to see the spot he was pointing to. Sure enough, the odd glow we'd seen creeping out from among the tree trunks was surely there and together we moved toward it. I'd seen the effect several times then, but I inexplicably began to wonder why it was happening, what it all meant, even what—or who—might be behind it.

My own house appeared before us. I was rooted in place, unable to look away, even if I wanted to, but I didn't because I knew what I'd see next.

There was my parlor and there was Roland James and Virginia Jordan sitting in it, talking. Rather, Roland was talking and as I listened in it seemed as if he was telling the girl a story.

"When will the séance begin, Mr. James?" Virginia interrupted.

"Why," said Roland, smiling, "it's already begun in a way."

Virginia clutched at her locket, her brow knitted in uncertainty. I thought to say something to them, but decided they would not be able to hear me…if what we were seeing was real at all.

Then, someone else was there in the room with them. A girl.

The phenomenon was abrupt; one moment she wasn't there, and then she was, or it may be that I simply didn't see her standing there before. If she had approached the scene, there was no movement that I detected, only the instant realization of her presence. A presence that neither Roland nor Virginia apparently recognized.

The girl looked to be perhaps sixteen-years-old or so, somewhat pretty with dark hair cut short, almost like a boy's, but more attractive than that. She was dressed so oddly, like nothing I'd seen in Jordan, or in the advertisements I'd seen from other places. The girl wore a skirt and blouse combination, not a full dress, and the garments were loose on her and low-waisted. It was not a slovenly look, but gave the impression of purposeful fashion, though none I was familiar with.

The most disconcerting thing of all was that her skirt ended just past her knees, leaving her lower legs and ankles quite bare.

This young creature stood just beyond my guests, but moreso near Virginia. Her face was pale—no, her entire body, clothes and all, was pale, as if all the color in her and her apparel had been leached out. Her face was composed and a bit sad, her eyes dull and lifeless. She gazed down at Roland and Virginia, I presume watching them, though there was little life to her.

148

All of a sudden I wondered if she was a spirit. But if so, wouldn't Roland realize her presence? I looked at the man and saw only that he continued to speak to Virginia and gave no indication he knew someone else was in the room. I wished I could somehow call out to him to tell him what I was seeing. And then it happened. Roland stood up abruptly, his eyes darting back and forth across the room, his head turning too while he held up one finger on his hand as a signal to Virginia to remain quiet.

Whatever occurred next I do not know, for the scene faded and the trees returned to end the moment.

Mr. Jones and I hurried away from the spot, an unspoken but mutual eagerness to return to the waking world.

When I was back in my home, sitting in my parlor waiting for Roland to shut the door after seeing the Negro off, I smiled to myself, thinking of the "impropriety" of my ghost-hunter being alone with me without a chaperone. The thought passed quickly, for I had something important to say to the man.

Firstly, though, he informed me that he sent Virginia away with a warning to limit her activities to only very ordinary things for the days to come, and to stay indoors as much as possible. I remarked that with her notoriety and her father's concern over it, that shouldn't be a problem. I also added that there may be the possibility of Clement Chase seeking her out.

"We'll add that to our list of worries, Valerie," Roland said as he sat down across from me.

His calling me "Valerie" again spurred me on to say what was on my mind, but first I told him of my journey down the Old Track with Raymond Jones. He didn't seem too overly surprised by it, but he was evidently moved by my recounting of the strange apparition of the girl in the room with him.

"It's something to do with the locket," I said, coming to the end of my tale.

"It's something to do with the locket," he agreed, nodding. "The connection is there, but I don't know who the girl is. And I'm guessing you don't either."

Without pause, I hurried on. "Roland, something is very wrong with all of us. With you and me and Mr. Jones.' I told him what the Negro had told me about the scene we'd all three seen in the summer. He sat back and intertwined his fingers over his chest, looking at me with his one good eye.

"Yes, you're entirely right," he said finally. "We are not just witnesses to all this, but have roles—active roles, I might add."

I asked him what we could do about it. I had no desire to continue the way we were, to let events carry us along. I didn't feel like myself and didn't like it. He sat forward again and reached out his hand, palm up. Surprising myself, I reached out and laid my hand on his without hesitation. The contact felt good, and it felt *right*.

Roland said "The key, I believe, is in this other puzzle, the mystery surrounding Virginia Jordan and Quiggley. We must solve that first before we can help ourselves. I feel very strongly about that."

We had never spoken about any ties between the Jordan girl and the old man, but when he addressed it I recognized he was most likely correct.

"I'll return tomorrow," he told me as he stood up to leave. "And we'll start putting it all together." Before he closed the door behind him, he asked if it would be all right with me to bring Raymond Jones with him then.

"Of course," I said. "He's in this with us."

October 5

As is turned out, we did not reconvene to continue our discussion in my home the next day. Rather, it was today and in one of the two restaurants in Jordan. One of them is a nice place with linen table-cloths and matching silverware, and the other is more of a café, a rougher-around-the-edges establishment with hodge-podge offerings and décor. In all honesty, it's become a favorite spot for most of us townsfolk, as well as a place where everyone may eat together in the same room, including Negroes.

Roland looked tired, I thought, and Raymond Jones the same. They both told me the dreams of trains or one particular train had returned and restful sleep was proving elusive. I wished I could tell them my own dreams had been devoid of trains for weeks, but just last night I rode one to the point of annoyance…and hours of insomnia.

"Ask the questions," Roland said as we sat down and settled in at our table.

I resisted the urge to glance around the room to see if I and my odd companions were attracting any undue attention, but told myself none of that really mattered anymore, not after what I'd been experiencing for months now. Instead, I composed my thoughts and sorted through them. Where to begin?

"Who was that girl?" I offered, the question popping into my head. "And how is she connected, if at all, with Virginia Jordan and her locket?"

Roland urged me to continue, obviously wanting to air the questions before we tried to affix them with answers.

My husband rose up in my thoughts. "Who are the woman and child in Quiggley's photograph? And how might Robert be in any way connected with them?" I paused, letting the questions seep into me, and then added "And what does George Honeywell have to feel so guilty about?"

"We need to talk to him about that," Roland said. "The sooner the better."

Raymond Jones spoke up, asking if *all* these people were connected somehow.

Roland nodded. "And we three," he added.

It made me very afraid just then, that idea, like it hadn't before. "You believe it has something to do with the way we feel?" I asked Roland. He shrugged, but not casually. He did so slowly, perhaps reluctantly. He is a man who doesn't like mysteries, or rather he doesn't like not knowing their solutions.

"We've left out a question," he said, looking to me and then to Jones. "I think it needs to be said, although we haven't truly broached it yet. Not consciously."

I could only stare at him, unable to answer, unable to say what he meant. The Negro must have felt the same, for he too only stared at Roland and remained silent. We made for a pretty trio, I thought; three people loaded down with questions and no answers.

"Who are we?" I offered after a full minute had passed with no one saying anything.

"Yes," replied Roland.

It was too much. I couldn't bear it...but it was as I said it. I'd been skirting around it, avoiding it, but I wasn't myself. I no longer felt like *me*. Roland calling me "Valerie" more than once was not just annoying—it sounded like it might be true.

I took a drink of water and began to talk, the words flowing out of me. "Quiggley, Robert, Virginia, the strange girl, the tracks... the dreams..." I looked right at Roland, thinking of how much my life had changed since he'd come to town. "None of it makes any sense, damn it."

He placed his hand over mine on the table. I should have removed it, but I didn't. I wanted an anchor, a rock, and he was as good of one as any in this storm.

"Marie, I truly believe we need just one piece of the puzzle to fit into place for us to see the larger picture."

Jones nodded, clearly in agreement with the man. I wanted to shout at him, tell him he was wrong to fall into Roland James' camp, but a voice inside of me urged total compliance with the ghost-hunter. And *trust*. I nodded myself, turning my eyes downward to the table so I didn't have to see any more truth in Roland's one good one.

"So," he said to us both, "let us go and see this caretaker."

October 10

Days passed before we were able to approach the caretaker of the Jordan estate, George Honeywell. I had heard he wasn't feeling well and I agreed with Roland that we needed the man in a better state than sickness if we were to learn anything from him.

This afternoon we walked together to the House on the Hill— myself, Roland and Raymond Jones—and talked as we went along. The subject quickly turned to Virginia Jordan and her situation.

"Why do you think she went along with Chase's capers?" my companion asked. "You knew her before her abduction; was there anything then to indicate the girl would ever do such a thing?"

I thought long and hard before answering, and found the ideas forming in my head dark and reprehensible.

"Virginia was a lonely child," I told him, choosing my words carefully. "She was particular about those to whom she attached herself, though—still, if someone were charismatic enough..."

Roland shook his head ruefully. "I see. It does happen, of course. In war, especially, and in other circumstances, too."

I began to ask him what he meant by that, but the cold realization of it was already there in me, no matter how much I was avoiding it. *Good Lord, that poor girl.*

Roland sensed my distress, I'm sure, but he kept on talking as his thoughts on the matter unspooled. I listened, horrified.

"A prisoner who, well, becomes attached to a jailor...perhaps even intimate—" I stopped him right then and there to implore him not to continue. He patted my arm consolingly as my stomach roiled and my head ached at the very idea of that young girl, snatched from her home, bundled up to who knows where, subjected to...and then to... It's simply inconceivable, but what else makes sense? I tried to speak what I was feeling inside, but I couldn't. I just couldn't.

"And why then would she leave him?"

Thankfully, any response I might have mustered to the question was moot as we came up to the lovely iron gates of the House on the Hill, made with care and craftsmanship by the Jordan Ironworks, the founder of which resided in the estate we gazed up at. To my surprise, two men stood by the gates, both armed with pistols and rifles.

I have never seen guards at those gates before, armed or otherwise. We had previously agreed that Jones would stay back and out of sight. Though Russell Jordan had employed Negroes in his company, we couldn't be sure that his caretaker was as open-minded on the subject. Roland walked up to the gates, hailed the men, and introduced himself and his purpose. The men were immediately wary and held their rifles in a way that suggested they could have them pointed at my companion without a moment's notice. Undeterred, Roland pressed on, explaining we only wanted a word with Honeywell, not with any member of the Jordan family. As he spoke he kept both his hands clearly visible at all times and did not make any abrupt movements. It occurred to me he'd done this sort of thing before. The guards were not impressed and told him that under no circumstances were they to open the gates for anyone at all, save those Mr. Jordan specifically wanted to see and had given their names to the men—thank you, sir, and be on your way.

I listened to the entire exchange, although I stood back several feet from the gates. The men did not look my way or even glance at me; I was nothing to them.

Something bubbled up inside of me and as Roland stepped back from the gates and began to turn toward me, I shouldered past him and addressed the men. They tried to interrupt me, but I wouldn't allow it. My words lashed out at them in a tone and voice I did not recognize, telling them who exactly I was and what exactly I required and did Mr. Jordan need to know they were not being cooperative?

The men looked at me dumbfounded and then tried to speak, but managed only to stutter out incoherent babble. I kept up my vituperation of them, keeping them off-balance as my volume rose and my anger soared. At one point it was as if I was up above myself, looking down on my body as it spoke unbidden by me. I was getting results, but I could not recognize myself.

Finally, one of the men assured me he'd go and get the caretaker if I would only be patient and allow him a moment to do so. "Be quick about it," I threw at his heels as he stalked off to the little cottage just beyond the gates and disappeared through its side door. Not thirty seconds later the man was back and unlocking the gates to tell me that my companion and I could go to the cottage for Honeywell, but please not past it.

As we walked up the stone path to the caretaker's home, Roland stared at me with an odd expression on his face. I asked him in a calm voice, my own, if I was possessed by demons.

"No, Marie," he said sympathetically, "of that I am certain. We *will* figure this out one way or another."

We soon found ourselves in the same room we'd seen while on the Old Track, and face to face with George Honeywell. He appeared to be sober, but perhaps only slightly.

"Hello, Mrs. Randolph," he said from a sitting position at his table. "Yes, I recognize you, but I don't have anything to say to you. The guard at the gate said you were off on some tear and wanted to see me—can't imagine why." He looked Roland up and down and didn't like what he saw, apparently.

Believing it was up to me to make the first sally, several gambits played through my mind and I chose one at random. "I'd heard you've been unwell, Mr. Honeywell."

The man looked at me in disbelief. "Can't imagine where you heard that from, ma'am. And besides, even if it were true, why would you bring fire and brimstone down on my man out there over it?"

Roland stepped up beside me and laid his hand on my arm. "Did you know a Mr. Quiggley, sir?" he asked. "From the Ironworks?"

The caretaker was almost instantly nervous at the question and his eyes roamed over the table and to a nearby shelf, most likely seeking drink. "That's none of your business," he replied, but without any teeth in it.

Roland took a step closer to him. "I see you've been a military man," he observed, pointing at a photograph on the mantle over a fireplace, one I'd completely missed when we stepped into the cottage. It showed a much-younger Honeywell in uniform, standing with several other men of the same youthful age. "Were you in the same regiment with—ah, yes; here he is, Mr. Quiggley...Corporal

Quiggley, then, if I'm reading his rank correctly."

Instead of protesting as I expected, the caretaker sobbed and lowered his head to the table. I felt sorry for him, but we were in such need of information. "Doesn't matter anymore," he muttered in-between sobs. Then he raised his head, his face frozen in a rictus of fear and shouting "He'll *haunt* me, he will! He'll *haunt* me 'til *I'm* dead!"

I wasn't sure what to do. Looking at Roland, I implored him with my eyes to do something, say something, anything, to the man to ease his pain. I was no longer the woman who thrust a hot poker between the bars of the gates to get my way; I couldn't stand to hear and see Honeywell in such a state.

Roland stepped over to him and stood at his side, looking down on the shell of a man that sat there. "No, Mr. Honeywell," he told him, "he won't. We took care of that. He's moved along and cannot hold anything over anyone here on this plane anymore."

The caretaker's sobs quieted somewhat and he turned to look up at my companion with questing eyes. "Are you—are you a God-fearing man, sir?" he asked in a tremulous voice. Roland assured him that he was. Then Honeywell looked over at me to ask me the same question, to which I gave him my warmest assurances. He nodded and turned his head to stare ahead at nothing. This went on for a minute or so before he finally spoke again.

"I let him in,"

Dread flowed in, a familiar feeling, an old friend these last few months. I walked over to him and knelt down beside his chair. I asked him who he meant in a tone meant to convey safety and security.

"Quiggley,' he said shakily, "and…that man."

My heart skipped. I looked up at Roland, who himself looked stricken, too. "Do you mean the criminal Clement Chase?" Roland asked, his good eye narrowed, one hand rising up to touch the patch over the other eye.

Honeywell nodded and dropped his head, teardrops falling into his lap. "He said I *had* to, or he'd tell…tell about what we did back then, in the war."

All in a great rush, the scene changed. The caretaker sprang up and whipped around to face us both. "But she's *back* now! The little miss is back now! And you say the old man is *gone*! Good riddance!"

Roland attempted to interject, telling Honeywell we needed more information, that he was guilty of a great crime and furthermore—but no. The man screeched at us to leave, that he'd deny it all, and that we hadn't a leg to stand on.

"Get out of my home!" he shouted, spittle leaping off his lips. "And I'll tell Mr. Jordan and the little miss to have nothing to do with you ever!"

We left. There was nothing else we could do. We gathered up Jones, updated him on what we'd learned, and began to walk without a destination in mind. Or so I thought; our ghost-hunter had other ideas.

"We need *more*," he hissed as he walked. "We're very close to something now. Quiggley knew Chase, and as incredible as it sounds, *helped him abduct the Jordan girl.*" He stopped and spun around to face me and Jones. "Why? For the love of God, *why*?"

I heard every word he said, but couldn't make my brain sort it all out. I was still befuddled and off-balance by what I'd said and done at the gates, and of course, my concern for Virginia and her safety. She was back in Jordan with her father, but Chase was still out there somewhere and the Lord only knew if he might have more accomplices to help him secure her once more.

"The Old Track," Jones suggested. Roland dipped his chin to look down at his own boots, contemplating the idea, I reasoned. He then lifted his face again and told us it was a worthy suggestion and that he thought we should go right to it.

On the way to the spot, he explained an idea that had occurred to him. "We have always allowed the Track to show us what it will. I am of a mind to ask—no, *tell* it what we wish to see."

I asked if that was possible. "Much is possible, Marie," he replied, hurrying us along, "if we at least make the attempt. And I am now of a disposition to make that attempt. Things are coming to a head, unless I've misunderstood the signs, and I'm of no mood to let events progress at the same pace. We must speed things along."

I wanted to inquire as to what end, but I remained silent and increased my own pace to try and match my companions. Jones also remained very quiet, and I could tell he was both in deep thought and following Roland's lead.

Once past the hillock and to the edge of the woods, I stood between the two men and willed myself into the glade. The ingress felt different somehow, and once inside the place the feeling was much headier. The air itself was thick with something, and darker, and the figures that normally capered just around the edges of my vision were absent. I remarked on this to Roland, but he was of singular mind and urged us down the track and under the great canopy of trees. The silence of the Old Track was never more deafening.

Roland began to call out "Hear me! We have a very great need!" I bit my lip in apprehension as he did so, the sense of, well, *changing the rules* overwhelming. Something was building in the glade, a presence we'd never felt before. My companion continued to call out, his voice tinged with frustration and a bit of anger, and I worried he might be somehow taking things too far—I had often felt like an intruder on the Old Track, tolerated but not necessary to the existence of the place.

Raymond tugged at my sleeve and pointed ahead of us. When I saw what he'd indicated I drew in my breath, loud enough to draw Roland's attention. Both the Negro and I pointed down the rails at the apparition that approached.

It was a great train, larger than any I'd seen before, a monster of a locomotive all black and smoky and ominous. It came down the tracks silently, which made it all the more sinister and otherworldly. We stood and watched it come, mesmerized, until I remembered how close we were standing to the tracks. Then, in an instant, it was upon us. One flicker of the light and it jumped ahead on the tracks; another and it was so close to us I could reach out and touch it.

"I wouldn't recommend it, Marie," Roland said, and I looked to see that I'd stretched out one hand with fingers wide, the tips of them mere inches from the black iron and steel of the locomotive. I jerked it back, wondering what in the world I was doing.

Together we took several steps back from the phantom train and looked down its length to the first car past its load of jet-black coal. Roland exclaimed "Good Lord!" and with one, swift motion swept one arm around to push me back and stepped in front of me. I peered over his shoulder at a vision straight out of the Pit.

A figure came down the steps of the car, slowly, assuredly, cock-of-the-walk. I say a figure, but to my eyes it was a great plume of smoke that billowed around something that wasn't there, and in effect defined it—the figure of a man. The hair on my neck and arms stood up as I stared at the thing and it stepped off the train car and alighted on the ground. It stood there for a moment, an undulating column of smoke, and then turned to look right at us.

The figure gave a little jerk of reaction, and began to walk our way. "*Run*," Roland hissed at us.

The two men wheeled about and began to run. I am a woman and I wear dresses. They are long and have many layers to the skirting. I grabbed at my skirts, lifted them, and tried to run. Three strides and I was pitching forward, the ground rushing up at me. Hands snatched at my arms, pulled me back from falling face-first onto the rough soil around the tracks. I felt something knock my heels and suddenly my shoes were off my feet and I was nearly flying across the ground between my two companions.

We moved quickly, but I felt it would not be quick enough.

"It's Chase," Roland told me, and my heart pounded in my breast, fit to burst. I could hear Raymond breathing hard as he both pulled and carried me along; likewise, Roland did the same, but I caught a glimpse of him turning his head to look back at our pursuer. Ahead of us, the spot of transference could be seen, but I feared we'd never reach it.

The glade grew dark, just as if storm clouds rolled in, and a strong wind began to blow, not favoring us, but impeding our flight. A shot rang out. There was no mistaking it as anything but a gunshot. Roland yelped and his body spasmed, but he did not let go of me. I began to pray.

We reached the spot and turned as one, linking our arms together.

I squeezed my eyes shut, not wanting to see the apparition of the man heading toward us, but to concentrate on the one thing that could save us: returning to the outside world. I wrenched my mind off our predicament and said over and over again how much I wanted to be home. Somewhere, I heard Raymond's voice, but not Roland's.

Then, I was falling. The sensation of transference had never felt like that previously. I fell to the ground with bone-jarring impact. Something fell atop me, but I could not move to see what it was. I realized there was sun coming down on me, and I knew we were out.

We were out.

Someone was calling my name and then Roland's. I tried to roll over, but something heavy was still lying on top of me. Finally, the weight lifted and I turned to see the Negro cradling Roland in his arms, tears streaking down his dark cheeks. I asked what it was, what had happened, and looked around to see if the gunslinger was with us.

"It's Mr. James, ma'am," Raymond said, and repeated it. "He's bad. He's in bad shape. Oh, my Lord, he's in powerful bad shape."

Every bone in my body aching, I struggled to sit up and looked at the two men to see both of them stained by bright, red blood.

"He's shot, ma'am," Raymond cried. "He's shot, and I think he's dead."

Winter
THE QUESTION OF ANSWERS

December 18

Weeks have passed. Winter is coming. Roland James is not dead. Earlier today I looked at the calendar and those were the three thoughts that came to my mind, that and I wanted to write this down.

Roland is not dead, but he is injured. How exactly he is injured and to what extent I cannot say. When we got him into my house I examined him quickly and discovered that while there was much blood on him, I could find no gunshot wound or any other kind of wound for that matter. He had every sign of great blood loss, but nothing on him that the blood could have escaped from. And he has slept or been in a catatonic state since that day. I have cared for him all this time, day in and day out, and he hasn't gotten any better, or any worse, also. I would say it's very strange, but everything about and around this man is strange.

I also found my sense of knowing what to do with a wounded person strange, as if I'd often been around the injured or guns that cause injury, but I have consciously never experienced those things.

Raymond Jones has helped me as much as he can, and I've found I can trust him. He appears to be a good man, and as bewildered as me over these events that dog our heels. After the first two weeks of taking care of Roland, I invited him to feel free to sleep and eat in the little shed on my property, the building Robert used to call his "den." It has a fireplace and a bed, and Raymond tells me he's made it quite cozy for himself.

He knows that for a long while I fought an urge to be dismissive of him, to treat him differently than I treat others, but he has been very patient and tolerant with me. If truth be told, I'm so very glad to have him close at hand. You see, we do not know where Clement Chase is. There has been absolutely no evidence of the apparition we saw on the Old Track, though we have kept watch for it these many, many weeks. At first, we believed the things would come crashing through a door or a window at any moment, firing its spectral re-volvers at us, but when days passed and nothing happened, we began to wonder what we had witnessed in the glade.

Raymond voiced it first, wondering if Chase was actually dead, though it seemed as if what attacked us *was* a spirit or ghost. With a clearer head after escaping from the glade, I noted that I had never heard of the man being killed or dying, but of course he may have and the newspapers may simply not known to report on it. We both agreed we didn't imagine the spirit, and Roland was certainly hurt in some way, but without his knowledge and experience to guide us on all this, we feel lost. And so we have sequestered ourselves for the most part, only venturing out to secure food or wood for the fireplaces and to examine our surroundings for signs of Chase…and to keep our ears to the ground for rumbles of danger.

Virginia Jordan's safety was paramount, of course, but my thoughts often strayed to the other girl, the one I saw here in my own home. Was she a ghost, too? And if so, who was she in life? Why was she apparently haunting Virginia? The more I thought about her the more my concern for her increased, strangely enough, and to this moment I feel as if I am as protective of her as Virginia, which makes no sense to me. I know I need to make sure Virginia is unharmed and out of Chase's clutches, but so, too, is there a growing need within me to find that other girl and—what? If she is dead, she is beyond such a need for safety, isn't she? It was all very troubling.

To make matters even more troubling, I have heard from numerous sources around town of men being let go from their jobs at the Jordan Ironworks. There is a pall over the town, something different from the depression that normally sets in as fall ends and winter begins and we all begin to think of hunkering down for a long, cold stretch of months. No, it's more than that, I'm certain. Jordan is changing, and not for the better.

I awoke early this morning to rise and fix breakfast for myself, Raymond, and Roland, and as I did an idea crept into my mind, one equal parts ridiculous, foolhardy, and audacious. I tried not to focus on it, but it was a strong compulsion and as I cooked and cleaned I laid it out as a plan and made up my mind to present it to Raymond.

"I believe we should try to determine whether that thing on the Old Track is still there or not," I told him as he finished his breakfast. "By going there to the glade."

163

To his credit, he did not look or act alarmed. He simply looked at me, closed his eyes for a moment, reopened them and looked at me again before he spoke.

"Why, Mrs. Randolph?" he asked. I told him he may call me Marie when we are alone, but he insists on "Mrs. Randolph" or just "ma'am."

I told him of my concerns and that we will never feel secure until we know for certain the hateful apparition is gone. And, I added, when Roland awakens, we'll have good news for him.

He didn't like the idea, though he hid it well. In this and in some other slight ways, Raymond reminds me of Robert, of all people. He got up from the table and paced a bit, clasping his hands together over and over again. Finally, he stopped, turned to me, and said, "Yes, ma'am, I believe you're right. I should take a look."

It was just as I'd guessed; he had no intention of including me on the investigation of the Old Track, but I quickly reminded him he'd never get in by himself. It would take two of us, and Roland was in no condition to go.

Raymond nodded soberly and asked me when we should go. I thought on that for a minute, and a date popped into my mind: The first day of Winter, which just happens to be Robert's birthday this year. It seemed right somehow, though consciously I couldn't put any reasons behind it. Maybe Robert put the date into my head.

With our plan in place, we went about the day as normal, though we were looking ahead at an enterprise that was anything but normal.

December 21

Two men trudged across my backyard through the light snow of the first day of winter, except that it wasn't two men. One was certainly a man, a stout Negro, but the other was me.

I thought it through last night as I lay in bed trying to sleep and this morning when I arose I set about fashioning an outfit I could run in. The last time I was in the glade of the Old Track I needed to run, and though I fussed a short time over dresses and skirts that might allow it, it came down to a burst of frustration over not being able to wear pants as a man does. But then I thought, why couldn't I?

I went through Robert's clothes and found a pair of older pants that, while too large overall for me, could be belted in tight to my waist and rolled up at the cuffs. I added one of his thick workshirts, a winter jacket, a cap to keep my hair contained, and dependable pair of gloves. My ensemble complete, I met Raymond Jones by the shed and silently dared him to say something about how I looked. For the most part he declined to comment, though as we walked he began to say "ma'am" but with a slight smile changed it to "sir." I believe I also saw Mrs. Soames peering through her curtains at us, and I wondered what she thought she saw—most likely two strangers traipsing over my property.

The wearing of pants was a liberating sensation. It emboldened me as we neared our destination, the now-almost completely obscured tracks by the hillock. As two men, I felt as if we might just accomplish our goal after all.

The plan was simple in that very little plan existed: We were to transfer to the Old Track, take the lay of the land, and then return with no dallying. We agreed in advance that we were to remain tightly focused on the objective, to ascertain Chase's presence in the glade, and to leave immediately once achieved. Upon reaching the edge of the woods and turning our backs to the trees, doubt entered my mind almost immediately and my focus wavered as I mentally lined up the tracks. This, I now see, was our undoing.

I realized something peculiar was happening during the transference, but with no way to communicate it with Raymond, I steeled my nerves and prayed we were not heading into the face of danger—or worse. Opening my eyes, I saw there was an immediate difference from all the previous times I'd gone to the Old Track: I was not looking at foliage, but at the glade itself. The sensations were similar, but I discovered I could not move, which sent a jolt of panic coursing through my body. If we were frozen, we were sitting targets for Chase. We were essentially dead.

Then it became clear what was happening. I was *looking* into the glade, but not *going* into it, if that makes any sense. I wondered if my lack of focus, my wandering mind, caused the difference, but I pushed that aside to concentrate on what had been presented to me. I could see—I presume Raymond could, also—the track and the cathedral of trees, and I thought perhaps our goal could still be met. A sliver of confidence inserted itself in my thoughts; perhaps we were safe from the deadly spirit if we were not actually physically present in the glade.

To my eyes, everything looked much the same as always; the track, the trees, and the ground, but the dark pall still hung in the air there. After a moment, I saw why.

The smoky apparition appeared far off down the track, and as it moved toward us it began to coalesce into something more solid-looking, a man in a hat and with guns on his belt and walking with a slow, steady gait. Pure evil emanated from the dark figure, and I shrunk from it immediately. Then, as it came closer, strange sensations came over me: overwhelming *rage*, an anger so strong it felt like a fierce storm blowing in my face. Nothing moved in the glade except for the image of the man, but it projected such hate, such incredible ire, that I wanted nothing more than to remove myself from the place altogether.

It walked on, moving closer and closer to us, or what I perceived was our position, though I couldn't be sure we were not just looking in at the scene. The projection of anger continued unabated, but mingled with it I began to feel something else...despair. I can only describe it as a measure of sadness, of longing, and of great desire

166

that could not be sated. The mixed emotions overwhelmed me, and I may have sobbed from the tumult of them.

A pressure on my arm brought me around to realize Raymond was somehow reaching out with his hand to notify me of—the figure jumped and was instantly only several yards from us. It looked up, looked *right at us*, and I knew with utter certainty we were undone. It *saw* us somehow, perceived we were there and rushed in to meet us head on.

I willed myself back to the real world, calling out in my head to Raymond to go with me, to exert whatever will power he could to take us back before, before…

I was back. Snow on the ground, the air frosty, the hillock like a silent sentinel over the tracks; it was all there and I could move and see my breath puffing out before me in an icy cloud. I turned to Raymond to rejoice, but he had his back turned away from me, a large figure with his head bowed, impassive. I placed a hand on his shoulder—perhaps he was affected by the transference.

He wheeled around suddenly and my midsection exploded in pain. I doubled over, spitting out my breath in an explosive ejaculation. Something had hit me in my abdomen, something hard and with great force behind it.

As my knees betrayed me and I crumpled to the snowy ground I knew all at once that Raymond had punched me with his fist.

I couldn't comprehend what was happening. I trusted him. We had been through much together. Blood seemed to tinge the edges of my vision as I gasped for air, unable to even say his name. As I fell over on the ground I saw him walking away from me and toward the house, a dark figure, hands at his sides, fingers clutching and unclutching over and over again…

Consciousness left me, and for some time I lay there insensate.

Then, hands gripped me and shook my body. I heard someone calling my name and a face appeared before my eyes: Mrs. Soames, her entire countenance painted with shock and dismay. A roaring in my ears almost drowned her out, but when she managed to sit me upright, the sound diminished and I held up a hand to quiet her.

She asked me what had happened, what I was doing out there at the edge of my property, and should she send word to the constable?

I wanted her to do just that, Lord knows at that moment I did. Racked with intense pain and feeling betrayed, I wanted Raymond brought in and held accountable, but an odd little voice in my head told me to wait, think it through, and decide on it after I'd tended to myself and licked my wounds. Struggling to my feet I thanked my neighbor and informed her I was all right and would handle the matter alone. As I hobbled away from her in my men's clothing and my insides screaming at me, I must have appeared as an insane person to the woman. God only knows what she'd tell her husband the minister.

I eyed the shed as I passed it but saw no signs of life there. I was nearly to my back door when it occurred to me to look for Raymond's footprints in the snow, but thankfully when I did I couldn't see any that led to the house; only those of ours as we left there earlier. Once inside, I looked in at Roland and then fell upon my bed in extreme discomfort. Somehow, I slept for roughly two hours.

As I fell asleep I told myself how stupid I was to be playing at the game that surrounds me on all sides.

I awoke to mid-afternoon and looked in again on Roland. Stretched out on my sofa and wrapped in thick woolen blankets, he looked very peaceful. Though my entire body ached and a black bruise had spread across my abdomen, I sat down next to him and gazed at his face, wondering what I was to do next. Before I knew what was happening my arm was raised, reared back, and I dealt him a savage slap across the face.

Tears streamed down my face and I sobbed uncontrollably. Roland hadn't moved, hadn't reacted to my attack. I wanted to slap him again and harder. Anger welled up in me from my injured mid-section to spread throughout me, a righteous indignation with which I wanted to punish the man. But, despite my hell-bent ire, he just lay there, dead to the world.

Still crying, I leaned down to embrace his lifeless form and kissed his cheek tenderly.

Finally, I crawled back to my bedroom, wrote this all down, and fell back to sleep. Part of me wished it were for good.

December 22

I awoke with the sun streaming in my windows and the distinct awareness of someone in the house besides myself.

My mind went immediately to Raymond Jones. He didn't have a key so I wasn't sure how he got in, but I picked up a poker from beside the little fireplace in my bedroom and slowly opened the door to peer out into the larger room beyond. Seeing no one, but believing I could hear someone moving about in the kitchen, I moved stealthily through the door and across the floor, the poker before me and raised to do damage to the invader.

In the kitchen I found a very awake Roland James rummaging around in my cupboards.

Foregoing anything I could have said, I merely stared at him in astonishment. He asked if I intended to do him harm with the poker, and I assured him the thought had crossed my mind. Then he asked what the hell I was wearing, and I looked down to see I still wore Robert's clothes.

Minutes later, we sat across from each other at the kitchen table, food spread out before Roland and him eating one thing after another. I let him sate himself somewhat before informing him of everything that had happened since he'd been hurt. And to that point, he seemed to be completely well again. Even his color was back.

"Good Lord," he exclaimed, his one eye darkening, "it can only mean Chase has taken possession of our friend."

It was a conclusion I wouldn't have reached on my own, despite everything I'd experienced since the spring, but it made a kind of sense to me, and I felt the stirrings of relief when I realized the man was not in his right mind. Roland asked if I was all right, and I told him I hurt awfully but that I'd survive.

"More importantly, I think," I said to him, "what has been going on with *you*? At first we thought you were dead, and then we saw you were breathing, but there was blood all over you, though no sign of any wound and—"

Roland stopped me by reaching across the table and laying his hand on my arm. I covered it with my own hand and clung to it. After a moment, he spoke.

"Marie, something incredible has happened to me. I have been on an etheric journey."

I told him straight away I was done with games. I didn't know what that meant and wasn't sure I even cared. He needed to speak clearly and in words I could understand.

He swallowed that and digested it, then made another attempt. "In essence, I came out of my body. My—call it my spirit, my soul, my *etheric* being—came up out of me, this physical form, and I moved about the world, seeing but not seen, listening but not heard. I knew of the practice, of course; it is known throughout both the East and West, but to my knowledge I have never accomplished it myself. Until *now*. And it not only healed me from what I now know to have been psychical bullets, but it also *showed* me things."

He was smiling then. His was not a smile of happiness per se, but one of knowing, of gaining knowledge that bettered him. I asked him *what* things? Was it anything that could help us?

"Marie," he said, covering my hand with his other hand and squeezing it, "what I am about to say you won't find easy to hear. But, it needs to be said."

What could he possibly say, I wondered, that was more unbelievable than anything else I'd heard and seen since being in his company? I discovered with his next statement that there was still much for me to learn.

"Marie—we are *not* who we think we are."

An absurd statement, of course, but the words had a chilling effect on me: They somehow felt *right*. I opened my mouth to speak, a hundred rebuttals coming to mind, but I found they all sounded hollow. It was what I'd been feeling for quite some time.

"You and Raymond and myself," he continued, "these lives are a lie, or at least to us they are. I caught glimpses of many things as my etheric body travelled, but the one concrete thing I know is that we three are not these people. In fact, not even from here—and there's something about that I don't fully understand yet..."

I mustered a protest, finally. I told him I knew where I was from, who my parents were, my schooling, my marriage to Robert. How could it all be lies?

Roland frowned deeply. "We are all being punished for something—I'm not clear on what that is, but you and Raymond have obviously been given full histories. I have not been so lucky." He sighed and looked around the room. "Call it…hubris, I guess. Perhaps we have spat in the face of the gods, and are now paying the price."

Getting up from my chair, I walked over to the window to stare out at the wintry world. Roland was suddenly at my side, turning me around to face him and tipping my chin up to look him in the eye.

"Marie, I know you know I'm correct in all this. You've said as much to me before. The reasons behind it are relatively meaningless at the moment; we need to find our way back to our real lives, and I promise you that's just what we'll do."

It also felt right to embrace him then, and to cry on his shoulder.

"Come, now," he said presently. "We have to find Raymond—and protect Virginia Jordan from Chase. As such, the two things are not mutually exclusive. One will inform the other."

"I only pray we can do both," I told him and went to fetch my jacket, a sense of purpose once again motivating me and allowing me to set aside the very dark thoughts our conversation inspired. As we left the house, I glanced at the shed with trepidation that I might see signs of life there.

Roland steered us toward the House on the Hill. I looked around at my little town and thought it looked strange to me, as if seeing it for the first time. I tried to shake the thought from my head, telling myself my vision was skewed by Roland's pronouncement, but it only helped a bit. I couldn't help but feel it was all a sham and that I had no business being there.

Perhaps, I thought, it was for the best I was dressed as a man; more and more of Marie Randolph was slipping away by the minute.

We neared the Jordan home and could see people gathered at its gates, at the very spot we'd talked to the guards. Getting closer, I recognized our constable among the small crowd and dread once again crept into my soul.

Roland said he'd approach them first, seeing as how people might just recognize him, but not me attired as I was. I agreed it seemed a good idea, but when he'd stepped up to the gates, looked around, and then stepped back to me, his face was drawn and his mouth only a straight slit across his face.

"Blood on the ground there," he said plainly, "and lots of it. Someone has either been hurt badly...or killed outright."

I asked him if he believed something had happened to Virginia or her father, but he said he had no sense of it, only that pulling back and thinking our next steps through carefully would be our best course of action. We turned to leave the scene, but a loud, course voice called out to us, ordering us to stop.

My stomach dropped. Reaching out to grip Roland's hand, we turned around slowly to face Constable Stafford. The man was already glowering, but I saw his eyes dart to our clasped hands and his frown deepen—we appeared as two adult men, of course. Taking a step toward him I quickly raised my cap a bit from my forehead to give him a better look at my face.

"It's Marie Randolph, sir." I thought perhaps to smile, but didn't feel it appropriate for the situation. What in the world was going on?

Stafford's frown eased somewhat when he recognized me. "Oh, I see, Mrs. Randolph. Beg pardon, but I'm really after that man right next to you."

Roland stepped up and identified himself. The constable nodded and walked up to him, his eyes sizing him up. "Thought it was you," he said. "I'm looking for a Negro. A man. I think you've been in the steady company of one of late, isn't that right?"

"Yes, that's right, Constable," my companion replied. "I'd like to help if I can. What's this all about?"

Stafford sighed and glanced back over his shoulder. Back at the gate I could see a few of the people there had walked on and I caught a glimpse of dark, red blood on the snow just on the other side of the gate. "Matthew Grigg and Tom Packer have both been shot," the constable told us. "Matthew's in bad shape and Tom's dead. People have been hurt in this town before, fights and such, but never murdered outright. A Negro done it. He was seen."

Roland nodded solemnly. I wondered if his heart was pounding like mine. He told Stafford he hadn't seen his friend in a while, a month even, and then asked him what he was going to do about the killing.

"Have my deputies bringing in all the men Negroes," said the constable, his tone even and firm. "I thought maybe you could help with yours."

"Raymond is not mine, Constable. He is his own man."

Hoping to allay any tensions or suspicions about Roland, I chimed in to assure the constable we hadn't seen our friend in quite some time, but that we'd let him know the instant we did—*if* we did. That seemed to placate Stafford, and so we left the area swiftly, but not too swiftly. As we walked away, I couldn't help but cry; I knew both the men who had been shot.

"He's not in his right mind," Roland consoled me. "It's bad, very bad, I grant you that, but in the end he's not responsible for his actions."

It was very little consolation. I pulled up my collar against the cold and walked on, adamant on getting home to a warm fire and a chance to sort it all out before I went mad. For the hundredth time, I asked myself how much more of it I could take before it broke me completely.

My house came into view and I stopped dead when I saw it. Pointing at the smoke that rose from it, I looked at Roland to see if he saw it, too, but he had already quickened his pace and drove on toward my home. As we got closer, I saw the smoke issued from the shed's chimney, which to my mind was even worse than if it had come from the house.

"Wait there!" Roland shouted back at me as he jogged to the shed and right up to its door. I stood there numbly, praying to God to intervene somehow.

Roland put his ear up to the door and listened for a moment until standing up straight and knocking at it. Seconds later the door opened and my companion stared into the darkness on the other side of the threshold. Finally, he took one and then two steps into the shed and stood just inside the door. My heart stopped and I couldn't breathe as I watched him, expecting him to be dead in the next second.

Then Roland stepped backward, leaned out the door and waved at me to come to him.

I marched toward the shed mechanically, with no emotion. What would be would be. As I approached the door, Roland gave me a slight smile and motioned for me to look at the figure in the chair in the room beyond. It was Raymond Jones, and I could tell immediately he was himself again.

"It's all right, it's all right," Roland assured me. "He needs much rest, though. Let's let him be and we'll all talk in the morning."

I nodded weakly at him, gave Raymond a little smile of my own, and made my way to my home, my body quite cold and my head empty of all thought save to somehow get warm again.

Roland wished me a good evening and closed the door behind me.

December 23

As I lay down to sleep last night I reminded myself who I am, and in fact began to repeat it over and over again: I am Marie Bennett Randolph, I was born in Lloydsburg, my parents were Estelle and Francis, my brother is Neil, my husband was Robert...and so on until it lulled me to sleep.

Dreams came, just on the verge of nightmares. I was the other one, Valerie, and not only did I live in another place, but seemingly another time...

Over a very meager breakfast in a very cold house, I pushed the images from the dreams aside and forced myself to dress and make my way out to the shed. I was glad to see someone had started a fire in the fireplace there.

Roland opened the door before I'd barely knocked upon it and I entered to see Raymond sitting in the very same chair as last night and looking like he'd been through a literal hell. I asked him how he was, regretting such a silly question the moment it left my lips, but he smiled somewhat and said he was better and had things to tell me and Roland. Obviously the two men had not discussed anything the night before, and Roland was true to his word to let the man be and get rest.

Raymond took a deep breath and told us of his ordeal. He said the spirit of Clement Chase came over him all of a sudden and that he had no time to resist the invasion, even if he could. Once possessed, though, he said he struggled mightily and called on the spirits of his own family to help in the battle. In this manner Raymond believes he retained some of his own consciousness. This was both good, and very, very bad.

Chase's thoughts, as it were, were chaotic, filled with rage and hatred for everything, especially women. How I escaped his wrath with only a blow to my midsection I do not know; I could have easily been killed. Raymond went on to say that the anger was all-consuming, but in the middle of it was the longing I'd felt momentarily in the glade, the urge to find the girl and bring her back to his side. It drives Chase, apparently, an overwhelming mission that transcends, well, *death* itself.

Why her? I asked. How did the bandit settle upon Virginia Jordan? Raymond didn't know, but Chase was not above murder to retake her. Here he faltered in his telling and grew silent. I found great amounts of sympathy welling up in me for him, and though there was still something deep down that tried to prevent it, I let it flow over me and even reached out to lay my hand upon his arm in solidarity, one human being to another.

"I know I didn't hurt those men," Raymond said after sitting quietly for a minute or two. "Roland helped me to see that. I feel awful about it, just plain wretched, but that man inside of me's the one responsible. He's got to be stopped."

Roland assured him Chase would be stopped, and as soon as possible. I then asked Raymond why the spirit let him go—did he know?

"After the shooting," he answered, "there was a moment of Chase being...spent, I guess. Some of the anger had leaked out and it let me think. What I did then was to recite the Lord's Prayer, and that's when I suddenly realized I was alone in my head."

"He's godless, this one," Roland intoned as he stood and began to pace the floor. "Utterly and completely. He may have been so abhorrent of your beliefs, my friend—and pardon me, but also the color of your skin—that he decided then and there he couldn't stand to be that close to you anymore."

Raymond's eyes flickered to me for a moment, and he said, "No pardon needed, sir. Whatever it was, I'm just glad it's done and over and I still have my life."

There was one more thing he added, an answer to a question that at one time not so long ago would have been explosive, but now I couldn't see how it could help us in the task ahead.

"That Quiggley is this man's father," Raymond explained. "That's one thing I learned from him, if nothing else. He hates him something fierce."

Roland sat back down and looked at me, his good eye open wide as he consumed that morsel. "Quiggley's *son*," he said thoughtfully. "It all fits now. It's the lever that Chase used on the old man to get him into the Jordans' home—and Quiggley in turn applied pressure to the caretaker to help him. It was all borne from the men's military service, I assume…Quiggley most likely had the child out of wedlock."

"The photograph!" I exclaimed. "The woman and child: Clement Chase and his mother, whoever she was." Robert popped into my head then, and I made a leap to presume he might have been like a son to the old man, the son Quiggley *wished* he had, not the horrible monster he did have.

Roland clasped his hands together and said that we now know *how* Virginia Jordan was spirited away from her home, but not *why*, other than Chase's lust for what? A companion, someone he could groom, someone he could…oh, the horrible thoughts of Virginia's *tutelage* under that despicable creature returned and I was swallowed up by them.

"He likes to control people," Raymond interjected. "Likes to boss them around, make them do what he wants. He's nasty in that way."

A knock came at the door just then, and I jumped a little at its sound. Roland reached out to silence us all, and then whispered that it was most likely that the constable or his deputies had followed us and would be taking Raymond into custody. It chilled my blood even more than the wintery air.

The knock came again and Roland got up to answer it. He listened at the door first, then swung it open to find Virginia Jordan standing there, a look of confusion on her pretty face.

The girl stepped right into the shed and came to me, her arms outstretched. I took her into my embrace and asked her why she was there. She was not crying, but I could tell she was filled with sadness over something.

"We're leaving, Marie," she explained. "Father and I. Leaving Jordan, I mean. He says we can't stay, not with—with *that man* trying to find me." As she talked she looked first at Roland and then Raymond. When she saw the Negro she jumped and said "Oh!" but I assured her he was a friend and as concerned for her safety and wellbeing as Roland and myself.

"They said a Negro shot our guards," Virginia said wide-eyed. "Jordan is falling apart, Marie. Father says it can't be helped, but the most important thing to do right now is to leave and go somewhere I can't be found."

Visions from my dream came to me, Virginia's future in particular, and I hugged the girl tightly, the thought of it all too terrible to contemplate. Roland cleared his throat for Virginia's attention.

"I'm sorry to ask, Miss Jordan, but when are you leaving?"

"Tomorrow, by train," she replied, her face to my bosom. I loved her so much at that moment, as if she were my own daughter, yet Fate was weaving a skein none of us could alter, or so it felt then.

Roland smiled kindly at her as he laid a hand on her shoulder and gently turned her toward him. "Then come see us tomorrow, just before you leave, if you can. I know you've probably moved Heaven and Earth to come here now today, but do your best again tomorrow, will you?"

The girl looked from him to me and nodded. Then she was gone as if she were never there at all.

I asked Roland why tomorrow, why not say whatever it was we had to say today while she was with us? He sat down next to Raymond and placed his hand on the man's arm. "Because,' he said, "we have much to do with her that will not be easy. Most importantly, we need to get that locket from her. It's central to our mission here."

He looked at me, really looked right at me, then at Raymond.

"Don't you see?" he asked us both. "We need all the weapons we can to fight the coming battle—and tomorrow's a special day. It's Christmas Eve, my friends."

December 24

That today is the day before Christmas is a concept I cannot credit. I look around my house and there is no evidence of the holiday, nothing to note its presence like every year before this one has. I awoke early and wondered who I am, not if Robert would like his gift from me, or what hymns we would sing at midnight mass, or several other little things that made Christmas a day to look forward to all the year 'round.

Instead of all that, I rose, dressed, and prepared myself for the ordeal ahead. Virginia Jordan would arrive at any time, if she was being truthful with us when she said she would.

Roland and Raymond joined me in my kitchen shortly before noon and the girl appeared at my door about an hour after that, explaining that she and her father were packed and ready to leave on the two o'clock train, but she was able to slip away from the House on the Hill while he took a nap.

"The constable was by this morning," she told us while eyeing Raymond warily. "He said he was coming here today to talk to you. I'm sure he knows Mr. Jones is here."

Virginia looked pale and tired, but some color came into her cheeks when she spoke of the matter. It amazed me that a young woman such as the one standing before me had actually lived on the run with a criminal for years doing who-knows-what and was now flushed of face talking about the movements of lawmen in her little hometown.

"We haven't any time to waste, then," said Roland. He turned to the girl. "Miss Jordan, I'm afraid I need to ask you for that locket. It's very important you leave it with us before you leave."

Virginia's hand went like a shot to her chest where the locket lie under her blouse. Her eyes rounded in fright and she took a step backward, in effect directly into my arms. "Do you trust me, Virginia?" I asked her in the kindest, most sincere voice I could muster at that moment. "Mr. James doesn't ask this lightly, but...we believe we can help someone tremendously by having it with us."

She turned around in my arms to face me. "It's the girl, isn't it? The one I—I see in my dreams."

I nodded to her and kissed her cheek. It was cold, but soft. Roland stood up, but kept his distance. "Virginia," he said, "that girl—how do I explain this? She doesn't belong here. We're very sure of that. And when I say 'here,' I don't mean just in Jordan alone, but rather here in this world. She isn't part of it."

Virginia faced him, but stayed close to me. "I would, sir. Give it you, I mean, but I *can't!*"

I asked her what she meant, and she told us in faltering words that she has been unable to remove the locket since she came back to town. She'd tried many times to take it off, but something prevented her from doing so. Roland frowned and took a step toward her; Virginia, to her credit, did not flinch.

"Listen to me, young lady—I will take care of that now, but you must do as I say throughout the actions I will perform. Is that understood? I will protect you, but you have to do what I ask, and if you do, you will have saved a life and will be able to go on with yours in peace."

That last bit was something of a falsehood, or at the last a stretching of the truth. All of us have had premonitions of darkness ahead of the girl—but beyond that we *needed* to help the spirit in the locket. I am not certain that Virginia is doomed, but if she is, there's nothing we can do about it. Somehow, God help us, we can do something for the strange girl we'd seen right here in my home. This I knew for certain.

When Roland had us gather around a table, I knew he intended to contact the spirit of the girl. He arranged it with Virginia across from him, me to his right and Raymond to his left. I saw Virginia shirk a bit when she had to hold hands with Raymond, but she went ahead with it. I lowered the lights at Roland's direction and the circle grew quiet.

"Place the locket in the center of the table, Virginia," Roland said. The girl shook her head and said she couldn't even take it off from around her neck. Roland grimaced a little, but nodded and continued.

"I am calling out to the spirit within the locket. Please let us know you are here and willing to communicate with us."

There was no reply of any kind, or at least none that I registered. Roland frowned and closed his eye as if concentrating. "Something is not right here," he said. "This is not a kind of spirit I have dealt with before. It's almost as if..."

A thought struck me just then, one so strong I couldn't hold it back. "Her name is Laura," I said out loud. I knew it was correct, like the girl herself had told me directly. Maybe she did.

Raymond spoke up. "She is afraid. Very afraid."

"Why, Laura?" Roland asked, keeping his eye closed. "Why are you so afraid?"

Virginia looked adrift, her features pinched and confused. She appeared to want to speak, but also that nothing was coming to her. Finally she said "Laura! They can help you! Oh my lovely; they can help you, dear!"

"Yes, Virginia is right," Roland added. "You've nothing to fear. We will help you and protect you. Please don't shy away from us."

Another thought struck me. "She wants to go home." Tears came to my eyes; the statement was made out of great longing. "But she doesn't know where it is. She can't find it, can't see it."

Virginia squeezed my hand, hard. I suspect she was gripping Raymond just the same. "It's all right, Laura!" she cried. "Please let them help you! I will...I will *miss* you, but I can't help you."

Roland shook his head, his eye shut so tightly. "She's not dead. This is all wrong. The girl's not *dead*, not a spirit. She's trapped somehow. Incredible."

Something had been growing in my mind and I put voice to it. "Laura," I said, "let *me* take you! Will you come with me?"

Silence. No response. Finally Raymond spoke up. "She won't go with you, ma'am. She won't go with me, either."

I was thunderstruck, in a way. I thought we'd made some progress—why wouldn't she go with me? I concentrated and found...she, Laura, didn't *like* me. "Will you go with Mr. James?" I asked her, feeling desperation growing within me. "Will you go with him, Laura?

Something in the air around us eased, as if some pressure there was lessening. "Yes," said Roland, nodding. "She'll go with me." And then he released Raymond's hand and stretched his out across the table, palm up. Virginia looked at it, released my and Raymond's hands, and unclasped the locket's chain behind her neck. Looking at the silvery bauble with great sadness, she placed it in Roland's hand. Then, with tears streaming down her comely face, she got up from her chair, planted a sweet kiss upon my cheek, and ran from the house.

"If we're all in agreement," Roland whispered, "we can head to the station to see the Jordans off."

More than an hour later, the three of us stood and watched as Russell and Virginia Jordan climbed the steps up into a rail car and disappeared from our sight, most likely forever. We were standing off to one side in the station, at a vantage point that allowed us to see father and daughter, but hopefully not allow them to see us.

"I had hoped to ask Virginia about Clement Chase," Roland said. "If she knew whether or not he had really died. But, still, we have the locket, and we have Laura with it. That's the very best thing we could have hoped for...as well as Virginia away from this place."

"We shouldn't stay here much longer," Raymond offered. "The constable is still looking for me." He pulled his cap further down upon his head and turned the collar of his coat up. He looked at Roland for a reply, then to me.

"He's right," I said to my companion. "We should go, Roman."

The man turned to face me, his one good eye piercing me. "And with that...Valerie...it's time to go, yes. I couldn't agree more." He glanced at our friend. "And I believe Gabriel feels the same way."

Was it winter? It felt more like spring at that moment. Something had lifted off of me, off of all of us, and we knew we had to set the world—*our* world to right.

"Make whatever arrangements you need to," Roman told us, his hands on our shoulders. "Tomorrow, bright and early, on Christmas Day, we go home."

December 25

I did not sleep so much as I puttered around the house, "making arrangements" as it were, which is a joke when it comes to my life. My parents are gone, I have not spoken to my sibling in years, I have no real friends in Jordan, and besides—all of it is evidently lies anyway. Saying goodbye to Marie Randolph was very, very easy.

What was not easy was allowing myself to know "Valerie."

She would never have lived in a house this small and simple, apparently. She appreciates the finer things in life, having access to money, apparently, but none of it brings her any real pleasure or peace. She does things to fill in the holes, but they are superficial things at best. She cares for very little and holds even less close to her.

She does love this "Roman," though.

Oh, she tries to skirt around the subject, never really addressing it head on, but the feelings are there, the devotion, the sense that he somehow gives her life detail and meaning. She is her own person, regardless; I have no doubt of that, and in fact envy her a little on that score.

She doesn't care much for "Gabriel," but I may have changed her mind just a bit on that, enough to give her something to think about on the matter.

So that was my night: Walking around the house, thinking about all that, looking through Marie's things, holding pictures of Robert, putting everything in its place…then the sun came up and I dressed and made myself ready to place the largest piece of all in place.

I walked out to the shed with absolutely no recognition of it being Christmas morning on my mind, only thoughts of Laura and the locket and how at the very least we'd achieved her safety. I could feel good about that, at the bare minimum. Roland…sorry, Roman greeted me and invited me in, asking if I was ready for the journey ahead. I told him I was as ready as could be, for I had no real idea of what the journey entailed or what its destination was or how to get there.

"Home," he said in that calm manner of his. "Home for us all, down the Old Track."

Gabriel stepped up and reminded us that he didn't care to wait any more for Jordan's officers of the law to appear, so we bundled up and made our way out the door and across my property—Marie's property—and to the woods. We passed the first part of the track, now completely invisible under the snow, and then the hillock looking like some kind of white Christmas confection, and then the second part of the track, also unseen beneath the snow. We knew exactly where everything was. I looked at the treeline of the woods and even began to line everything up in my mind, trying not to think about it being the very last time. Somewhere behind me, across my backyard, sat my little house, my love nest with Robert, or so I believed.

We three stood in a row, side by side, gazing at the tree trunks, each with our own thoughts. Something prompted me to turn around before the men did—a sound? The snapping of a twig on the ground? A bird's cry? Whatever it was it brought me the image of a man coming around the hillock, a dark silhouette with the bright morning Christmas Day sun behind him, and carrying an unholstered pistol.

Constable Stafford.

Roman was already turned around when I looked to him, my heart frozen. I thought we could get away before being found, but someone might have informed the man as to...ah. Mrs. Soames, most likely, bless her. Possibly even by means of Uly, if she had sent the boy running into town to deliver the message.

"Constable," said Roman, raising both hands and taking a step toward Stafford. "Please allow me to explain something. It will be hard to credit, I know, but you must believe what I say when I tell you my friend here is innocent of the crime..."

I couldn't see how we would be able to talk our way out of being arrested, or at the least Gabriel being arrested. The explanation was purely unbelievable, no matter how one looked at it: Possession by a spirit, forced to do its bidding, including murder. I would have laughed if I could, but I saw only a bad end to it, for all of us. I began to think of what I could say to the man, words that might bring him around to listen to us and give us time to reason our way through it, but my mouth was dry as a bone and all I could do was play witness to the scene before me. In some ways I imagined it was much like what Roman described when he left his own body.

The constable was silent, covering us with his weapon and staring at Roman after stopping several feet in front of us right next to the train tracks. I tried to discern his face to attempt to glean something of his disposition, but the damned sun prevented me from seeing it clearly.

"It's not him," said Roman. I jerked my head around to see him, wondering what he was talking about, but almost immediately it dawned on me. It was Clement Chase.

A passing cloud obscured the sun just then, and for a moment I saw his face. Anger dominated it; pure, unadulterated rage telling the story of that which we'd robbed the bandit. The girl, Virginia, taken away from him again, still out from under his thumb, unable to be controlled and worse. But we hadn't, not really—we'd taken Laura, the other girl, and it was Russell Jordan had seen to it that his daughter...

A scream pierced the air. I looked past the constable to see... Virginia? *Oh, gracious God, please, no*, I thought, but it was true. All heads wheeled around to look at her running toward us over the snow, her hat sailing off her head, her bag forgotten and tumbling away, her mouth open and wailing, crying out, what? My name?

The gun. Chase's gun. It never wavered, though residing in the constable's body he'd made Stafford look over at the girl. The gun still pointed at us, his finger still tight on the trigger. Out of the corner of my eye something moved. I looked. Another gun rising up from somewhere. Gabriel. Gabriel had a gun, maybe one of the weapons he'd acquired to—to shoot the guards at the gates...

Virginia reached the constable and her hands were clutching at him, but in one swift move he deflected her with one arm and flung her to the ground, her momentum sending her sailing into the snow. A loud bang exploded right next to me and the constable's shoulder flinched and blood flew from it. Gabriel's shot had hit the man—no, not a man: Chase.

Roman shouted to not kill him, that it wasn't his fault. I presume he meant Stafford. Gathering all my wits, I sprang to Virginia to try and shield her, but as I did I saw Chase's pistol swing at me and he closed one eye to fortify his aim. A blur I believe to be Roman leapt at him.

Another loud explosion near me. I tensed for the bullet to hit me. In a wink I was shoved aside to go sprawling into the snow. A large dark figure had thrown itself at me, pushed me away: Gabriel. He closed up into himself, holding his body and falling backward. Roman jumped at Chase and they went down in a tangle of arms and legs. I thought Gabriel had to be dead, but the next thing I knew he was wrestling with Chase, too, trying to hold him down with Roman doing the same.

There was blood on the snow. Virginia was near it, but I didn't know who it belonged to.

The girl was screaming something over and over. I moved to take her in my arms, crushing her to me, telling her it was all right, all right. She wouldn't stop screaming and crying. I asked her what it was, what was happening. She looked at me, her features twisted in hysteria.

"He's my *father!*" she shouted. "He's my father..."

Time stopped. It simply stopped. I stared at Virginia, trying to comprehend what she'd said. It couldn't be. That wasn't how I'd seen it, how I had it in my mind, what I'd told myself to make sense of it all. Chase's *daughter?* Not his...not his...

The constable stopped thrashing in the men's grips. His eyes rolled up in his head and he moaned low and disturbingly. Suddenly he began to writhe around and shake, his back arching and his neck stretching in a way I didn't think humanly possible. Then, his mouth opened and a black mist sprouted from it, swirling like a miniature tornado.

"Back," Roman commanded, "back!" He let go of Stafford and scrambled to his feet; Gabriel did likewise. I saw blood dripping off him from somewhere.

Before it even could properly register on my eyes, the mist coalesced into the shape of a person, quite plainly visible with the white snow as a backdrop. It wavered in the air, but did not move. Where its face should have been, two crimson points of fire danced there like burning eyes.

It lifted one arm and pointed to Virginia.

Roman spoke up, loudly and clearly. "Are you a believer, Virginia?"

In my arms, shaking, the girl nodded and croaked "Yes."

"Your *father* is not, Virginia," Roman continued. "Pray for him."

Amazingly, the girl obeyed. Her mouth began to move, hesitatingly at first, but then more surely. I caught snatches of what she was saying: The Lord's Prayer.

The mist shifted, its other arm rising so both limbs were outstretched before it. Chase the bandit, the man with no god, the law unto himself, wavered and flickered in the air.

"Father!" Virginia called out, and I believed she meant God, but realized she meant her own father. "*Why?*" she screeched. "Why?"

"Keep praying for him, Virginia," Roman suggested as he took a step toward the figure of the bandit. His hand went to his face. "Pray for his soul."

The girl prayed. She shut her eyes tightly and prayed. I looked at Roman as he took another step toward Chase, until he was then right in front of the figure.

"Look at me, Clement Lee Chase," he said. "*Look at me!*"

Roman's hand went to his eye, his covered eye, and lifted the patch from it.

A horrendous scream filled the air, tearing at me. I have never heard a more terrifying sound in my entire life.

And then the figure was gone, as if it were never there at all.

January 1

As of today, for one full week, we have not been able to return to the Old Track. Roman says it is the only way for us to go home.

As each day has passed and our attempts to transfer to the glade are stymied, I have felt less and less like writing. Everything has become a strain on me and I feel as if I'm hovering in some kind of limbo between lives, Valerie's not feeling exactly right, but knowing that this one here in Jordan is wrong. So, in the meantime, I am trying to put down what has occurred since I last wrote.

We brought Constable Stafford to my house and watched over him until he awoke from his ordeal. Then, as carefully and gently and sympathetically as possible, we fed him small amounts of information until he had the entire picture. Even still, it was a bitter pill for him to swallow. In the end, he had to admit something completely untoward had been visited upon him and conceded that the same thing had happened to Raymond Jones. This was a blessing, I thought, one that allowed us the freedom to remain in my home while we tried to sort out our return to our proper existence. If what lies on the other end of the Old Track *is* our proper existence.

I have had several conversations with Roman on the subject, but I am not convinced.

My companion has stopped wearing his eyepatch, saying his eye is entirely fine. We have not talked about the disc that was hidden beneath it, the one with which he sent Clement Chase away...the one that has seemingly enlarged now since Roman has removed it from his eye. He keeps it in his jacket pocket at all times and cautions us to never look at its face, not even for a split second. Somehow I know this already.

Gabriel is my hero. He stepped in front of a bullet meant for me and suffered a flesh wound for his pains. I have cleaned it and dressed it, and it is healing well. While he recuperates, he has taken to reading from a book on trains that belonged to Robert, and appears to be thoroughly engrossed in it.

Virginia Jordan left here on December 26th and has presumably returned to...I was about to write "father," but I know now that Russell Jordan was never her father. She stayed overnight with us and slept with me in my room, and that evening we talked privately, woman to woman. She told me many things, albeit reluctantly at first, most of which I will not write here. One important thing I did learn was that he girl did fall in love with her captor and willingly joined him on his escapades, but when she discovered she was his daughter she was horrified and left him to return to Jordan. She struggled with the telling, but I let her say it in her own time.

I believe she is at peace now, or as much as she can be. On the morning of the 26th I urged her to go back to the man she grew up believing to be her father, and she agreed it was most likely the best course of action. As she left, I knew for a certainty I would never see her again.

On the third or fourth day of our failure to enter the glade, I walked to our little cemetery in town to visit Robert's grave. Covered in snow, it looked so serene and peaceful, but also strange to me, as if he was someone I'd only heard about or barely knew in life. As I walked back home I passed the Ironworks and saw it was shuttered. Jordan is dying from the inside out.

A few minutes ago, Roman told Gabriel and me he felt very good about our chances to make the transference today, it being New Year's Day. As he talked to us about the mediations he'd been doing over the problem the last few days, I felt a sense of encouragement and agreed it would be best to make another attempt. Gabriel nodded in his solemn way and told us he'd be ready to go when we were.

Perhaps it will work this time. If not, we shall try again, I'm sure. As I look around my house I realize how odd everything looks, like a place I'd only been visiting a short while, not my home.

Somewhere down the tracks sits my real home. I might very well see it before the day is done.

Part Three

THE LONG ROAD HOME

June 16th

Arthur,

We're on our way again! They have just told the passengers the train is ready to leave and we should prepare to board immediately— I can't believe it! It has been a terrible few days all together, but I'm glad they are done and I can finally come home. And maybe I will just stay a while this time and stop my gallivanting here and there.

Love,

Lydia

CROSS-COUNTRY LTD - 16 JUNE

TO: MRS. DANIEL CLOWERS
WEYFORTH, THE CITY

EMILY

EVERYTHING FINE NOW AND ON OUR WAY HOME.
TIME TO TELL VIRGINIA THE TRUTH AS A FAMILY.
ALSO WISH TO HAVE LONG TALK TO YOU ABOUT MY
CAMPAIGN. ALL MY LOVE.

DANIEL

Dear Granny Mima,

So much has changed, but so much so that I should tell you in person when I arrive there to visit you. It's not for letters that will never be sent, but for words directly to you where you rest. I will bring your favorite flowers and maybe a lunch basket.

I cannot stay long, though, because I do have a new job to go to. It's the same new job I told you of before, the one I thought I wouldn't take, but I've decided to step into it and make what I can of it. I have hope it will be a position of importance and of consequence, one that will allow me to work for a man of great distinction who often needs my help.

I will see you soon.

Love,

Gabriel

June 17

Dear Diary,

It has been four days since I last wrote in you. For me it has been
nearly an entire year.

I write this to you sitting in a car driving to Mount Airy, a trip
that has already been several hours. Roman is driving and smiling
because he likes to see me write. Funny thing: I can't recall ever having seen him write anything. Isn't that odd?

When it came time to return home and I steadfastly refused to
board the train—or any other one, for that matter—again, Joshua gal-
lantly offered to drive Roman and me to Mount Airy. After I reflected
upon his quaint little "flivver" and how we'd all have to cram into it,
I simply purchased an automobile of our own for the trip. Before too
long, Roman and I were on the road after saying our goodbyes to Gabriel. Some day I hope to sit down with him for a long talk.

As for Roman and I, we talked for quite a long time as he drove,
but he then grew quiet and contemplative so I've taken the opportunity to jot down a few thoughts of my own. I won't try to fill you in
on everything that's happened since I last took you up—that would
be more than I think I could apply myself to at the moment.

Mostly we have—or rather Roman has—discussed what he calls
the Dark Track. Here is distillation of what he has to say about it
since we've come back.

It is a "singular force of nature," and alive in some ways.
He approached it all wrong, and for that we paid a price.
It meant to teach us a lesson as to how wrong we were.
It will require "much more study" before he can use it again.

Again? Did I hear him correctly? I pressed him on that, but after
a brief silence he admitted he wasn't sure on that point. I might
have chastised him more, but I let it go. It was now completely in
his hands; I myself wanted no part of it. Roman, though, appears
wholly engrossed in the idea.

195

One thing we didn't speak of while we drove was the matter of our lives there in the town of Jordan and how much of it we should believe and take to heart.

Who was, or is, Marie Randolph? Did she ever really exist? I feel I know her as I know myself, but here now in the real world...I'm not certain. I can see her in my mind's eye, hear her voice, smell her scent, recall her home and everything in it, but the more I dwell upon these things they seem to slip away a bit, as if perhaps they were never real at all.

One thing I do know is that the town of Jordan is real. It exists. The story of Virginia Jordan and her dalliance with the criminal Clement Lee Chase is real.

But... she died. The girl died in a fire on the very train we were on; that much is a fact. I write that and I see it here on the page in black and white, but in my thoughts I see Virginia as a living, breathing person, a young woman full of life and dear to Marie Randolph. A young woman who could not live a lie at the side of a man who she came to think of as a lover, but discovered him to be her own father. The horror of it chills me even now.

Questions and doubts are consuming me, Dear One, and all I can think about is getting back to Mount Airy and begin to look into all of this. What did the Dark Track do to us? What did it do to the real story? Did it—did *we*—alter events that already happened? Is such a thing even possible? How did a *year* pass there when only a few days transpired here?

I want to ask Roman about it, but I'm afraid of what he might say. I'm afraid he might not have any answers himself. I'm afraid he might be as much in doubt as I am.

Clement Chase is gone, of that I feel certain. Roman's disc is absolute, if what he says about it can be taken as gospel. But if I don't have that to cling to, as ridiculous as it seems, what do I have?

Who is Marie Randolph?

I intend to find out.

Valerie

196

Dear Roman,

I know it has been quite a while since you've heard from me, since we returned from our journey, but I have been busy. I have been looking into the details of everything that happened to us.

Well, after a considerable investment of my money into an investigation, I cannot in any way determine that Marie Randolph ever existed, and for that matter, either Roland James or Raymond Jones, also.

Upon reaching this plateau, I made up my mind that nothing short of me going to the town of Jordan itself would do if I was to continue my investigation. Alas, that too proved to be an impassable wall.

You see, twenty-four years ago the dam outside Jordan burst and the town has been underwater ever since that day.

Roman, these sorts of things are your life, your calling, and your passion. You were very kind to welcome me back into that life after the dark days of your disappearance and the trial and all of that, but I find I can no longer be part of it, at least for now. I am a strong person and always have been; you know this, but I find myself on shaky ground every morning I rise from my bed and question everything around me...including you.

Please do not try to contact me, at least for a while. I need to determine who I am again, since the answer to the mystery of Marie Randolph seems to be forever out of my grasp.

I am very truly sorry, my love. Be well.

Valerie

GETTING BACK ON TRACK

It's been a long time
Now I'm coming back home

Those words from the Beatles were foremost in my mind when I sat down to write this piece, so with apologies to Lennon and McCartney, they seemed too apt not to open with.

This book has been a long time coming.

SGT. JANUS ON THE DARK TRACK was first announced in 2014 after the publication of SGT. JANUS RETURNS. "Sgt. Janus" was always intended as a series, and I had every intention of making it one as that announcement implied, but as Mr. Lennon noted many years after the penning of "Wait," "life is what happens to you when you're busy making other plans."

I dragged my heels getting started on DARK TRACK, and then some licensed work arrived and I got a big head over it and my creator-owned stuff sort of fell to the wayside. I had the book all planned out from the start. I knew the story, knew where it was going to go and end up; I "only" had to write it. But I didn't. Time passed. People stopped telling me they were looking forward to more Janus tales. Other occult detective characters from other writers took off and occupied many books of their own series. Janus receded into the past, but he was always in my mind, albeit in the back of it.

In 2018, after a very bad experience with a high-profile licensed novel, I pulled my head up out of the sand and tried to make a go at DARK TRACK. I wrote a few thousand words and set it aside. Then, 2019 arrived and I became far more acquainted with ghosts than I ever imagined or wanted.

Long story short, I was set on a new path in life and a new "normal." Early in 2020, I figured a story about Sgt. Janus doing just about the same thing was something I could do, having become intimately familiar with that general sort of situation. So I dusted off those few thousand words I'd written, looked over my notes—though the story had always been firmly etched in my brain—and hunkered down to finish it. For every single day of three months I wrote, no matter what, and got the damn thing done.

The story, as these things happen to writers, grew and transformed and became better as I went along. Valerie, my primary narrator, was always a part of it, but new characters got onboard as the train moved along and I was glad to make their acquaintance. Gabriel Butters in particular is now an immense favorite of mine and we *will* see him again.

Two things that evolved more than anything else from the original plot to the actual writing were the nature or essence of the Dark Track and of the town of Jordan.

Back when I thunk up the story, the Dark Track was basically a means to a way, a mode of transportation to get our Spirit-Breaker from Point A to Point B. As I got into it, the Track grew to take on almost a personality of its own, a nearly tangible thing that Janus struggled against. In fact, the Old Track in Jordan was originally a separate set piece from the Dark Track, but it became a sort-of extension of the Dark Track, a manifestation of it in Jordan that fit the landscape. I don't know about you, but I got seriously weirded-out writing about the Old Track—a surreal environment within a surreal environment, the town of Jordan.

Jordan was always a company town in my original plot. I'd somehow become fascinated with the idea of a company town several years ago, and I knew it would make an intriguing destination for the sergeant...but it was originally a lot less active than it is in the finished novel. Jordan was more or less a ghost town the way I'd conceived of it back then, with only a very small handful of people living there when Janus arrived. The whole idea of him arriving there roughly thirty years in its past and seeing it as a living town grew as I wrote, which is always a wonderful thing to happen to a writer.

Whether the entire second half of the story actually happened to our heroes, well, that's not clear to them, as you've seen. Oh, Jordan existed, but did Janus and Valerie and Gabriel alter time by being there? Or did they merely inhabit people who already existed there and lived out historical events? Perhaps they'll never really know.

I was very excited to be able to bring Joshua into the proceedings, albeit in a minor way. There are more stories about him flitting about in the ether, and I hope to get to tell them some day. He's a fun character to write, and I'm to understand he's become a ghost-hunter in his own right, or at least in his own mind.

So, where do we go from here? What's next for Sgt. Janus? I have ideas, of course. Long ago I revealed the fourth book would look at his path to becoming a Spirit-Breaker in his early days, kind of a "Sgt. Janus Year One" sort of deal. That said, I've recently discovered what happened to our sergeant after the events of DARK TRACK, and wow, what a tale.

Tell you what, chums: You tell *me*. Where do you want to go from here? As a certain Jedi Master once imparted, "Always in motion is the future." Sgt. Janus is back and there are spirits to break. Let's do this thing.

And thanks as always for being along for the ride.

Jim Beard
July 2020

ALSO AVAILABLE FROM

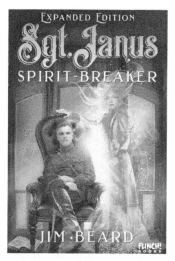

SGT. JANUS SPIRIT-BREAKER

"While he may deliberately conjure the spirits of authors of Victorian and Edwardian occult fiction before him, Beard's prose is fresh and entirely modern in his, at times, frank and unsettling tales of the wages of his characters' past sins. Each story breezes by and like the best tales told round the campfire, it leaves the reader hungry for more"

–William Patrick Maynard,
Blackgate.com

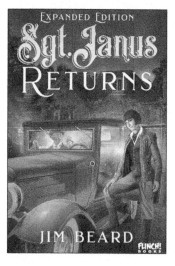

SGT. JANUS RETURNS

"A Modern Classic...This book is one of the best New Pulp adventures I have ever read. High praise? It's well deserved. I've enjoyed the author's past works but I really feel that he's elevated his game with this one. I simply can't recommend it high enough!"

–Amazon Review

ALSO AVAILABLE FROM

ALSO AVAILABLE FROM

FLINCH!
B O O K S

RESTLESS: AN ANTHOLOGY OF MUMMY HORROR

Six stories chronicling the ancient dead from around the globe who reemerge from the tomb to mete out a dark vengeance and balance the eternal scales.

"If you love old-fashioned horror…dim the lights and sit down for an evening of reading pleasure."
–Ron Fortier, Pulp Fiction Reviews

QUEST FOR THE SPACE GODS: THE CHRONICLES OF CONRAD VON HONIG

This world-renowned yet controversial author will search every inch of the globe to find the truth about ancient aliens …or die trying.

"If you thrilled at the notion of ancient astronauts as a kid of the'70s, von Honig's travels will have you longing once more for an interstellar brotherhood to which humanity might one day aspire."
–Amazon Review

Available on
AMAZON.COM
and
BARNESANDNOBLE.COM

ALSO AVAILABLE FROM

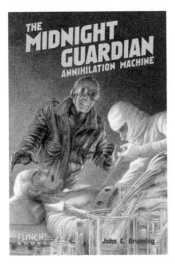